"But you said I wasn't your business anymore."

Grae brought his full weight down upon her. "When will you stop taking everything I say so literally?"

Tielle relished the brunt of his body against hers and savored the sensations he stirred.

"Don't do that." Grae bowed his head, whispering the order when she moved against him in a slow, needy grind.

"Do what?" Tielle bit down on her lip and moaned close to his ear.

He grunted what sounded like a curse. Loosely cupping her neck, he used his thumb to tilt back her chin. Tielle followed through on giving him her tongue and didn't know which one of them whimpered first when their tongues tangled, engaging in a sultry duel.

Tielle had lost her cap during the unorthodox trip through the house, freeing her coarse locks. Grae gathered a fistful of the dark mass, using his hold to keep her mouth crushed beneath his. She kept her hands filled with the material of his shirt, eager to take him out of it and paying little heed to what she was doing. She only wanted this—wanted him.

Books by AlTonya Washington

Harlequin Kimani Romance

A Lover's Pretense
A Lover's Mask
Pride and Consequence
Rival's Desire
Hudson's Crossing
The Doctor's Private Visit
As Good as the First Time
Every Chance I Get
Private Melody
Pleasure After Hours
Texas Love Song
His Texas Touch
Provocative Territory
Provocative Passion
Trust In Us
Indulge Me Tonight

Harlequin Kimani Arabesque

Remember Love
Guarded Love
Finding Love Again
Love Scheme
A Lover's Dream

ALTONYA WASHINGTON

has been a published romance novelist for ten years. In 2013, her Harlequin Kimani Romance *His Texas Touch* won the *RT Book Reviews* Reviewers' Choice Award for Best Series Romance of 2012. In addition to being an author, AlTonya also works as a college reference librarian. Her Harlequin Kimani Romance *Provocative Passion* was nominated for an AMB Ovation Award for Outstanding Interracial Romance and is the follow-up to *Provocative Territory*.

Indulge ME TONIGHT

ALTONYA WASHINGTON

HARLEQUIN® KIMANI™ ROMANCE

To Lost Loves and Loves Rekindled...

Recycling programs
for this product may
not exist in your area.

ISBN-13: 978-0-373-86372-3

INDULGE ME TONIGHT

Copyright © 2014 by AlTonya Washington

For questions and comments about the quality of this book please contact us
at CustomerService@Harlequin.com.

HARLEQUIN®

Printed in U.S.A.

www.Harlequin.com

Dear Reader,

Graedon Clegg and Tielle Turner are about to celebrate the worst milestone ever: the anniversary of their divorce. What's worse? The ex-spouses are set to spend a "fun-filled" week with Grae's family at Tielle's retreat for a little bonding time. Did I mention that the family hates Tielle for going through with the divorce even though Grae was the one who initiated it? I love to display the family dynamic in my work. Usually, the families get along—not the case in this particular tale.

It was a treat to portray Tielle—strong, self-sacrificing yet oh-so-much in love with her ex—and Graedon, the protective alpha male who bows down to no one…except Tielle. Peeling back explosive issues and working with such an outspoken secondary cast in such an intimate environment as Tielle's lavish retreat was especially delicious. I hope you'll enjoy indulging yourself….

Blessings,

AlTonya

altonya@lovealtonya.com
www.LoveAlTonya.com

Chapter 1

Vancouver, British Columbia

Tielle Turner looked away from the multicolored planning calendar that was projected on the farthermost wall of her office. The small plasma screen in the corner of the room's living area had droned on softly, offering no real cause for interest until Tielle's keen hearing picked up on the word *snow*.

She groaned.

"Is she kidding?" Tielle's round, coffee-colored face twisted into a glower, which she directed toward the woman who was delivering the midday forecast.

"It's only a *prediction,* Ti." Laura Cooper didn't bother tugging her dark eyes away from the wall projection she was studying. Laura had worked for her in some form or fashion for almost five years and was seemingly used to her mood swings whenever a discussion of the weather's quick change conditions was on the table.

"Sounds like it's for later in the week, too. No worries." Laura's eyes moved away from the projected calendar. "Besides," she called to the tiny woman standing in front of the TV with her fists perched defiantly against her hips, "it *is* autumn."

The reminder encouraged Tielle to turn her back on the television. "Autumn," she parroted with a smirk. "You know, when I think of autumn, I imagine leaves changing color and dropping from trees, the air turning a bit brisk, and the time changing. I imagine all kinds of descriptions. Ones she could give—" Tielle cast another tiresome look at the meteorologist "—but rarely does."

"It's Vancouver…" Laura turned back toward the wall.

"And that's why I live here. *Because* it's Vancouver." Tielle's vibrant eyes, the color of chilled cognac, glistened, and she seemed more appreciative of Laura's reminder that time.

"Vancouver autumns are supposed to be awesome." Tielle used a green dry-erase marker to point past the office's bay windows along the back wall of the office. The spotless glass offered a stunning, colorful array depicting the glory of the season.

"Well." Laura had pulled her attention from the wall again and was tapping her own dry-erase marker to the curve of her jaw as she treated herself to the view. "Since we *do* have such awesome autumns, aren't we entitled to have a few not-so-awesome ones?"

"Being cooped up with a group of execs isn't going to be fun for long if it snows, you know?" Tielle gave a conceding smile.

"I don't think it'll come to that. The Korman Group will be gone in two days," Laura said with a half shrug.

Tielle slipped the marker into a back pocket of her skirt and looked back to the wall projection she'd abandoned for the weather report. "After Korman, we've got offers from four more corporations for weeklong retreats.

And if this snow hits…" She let the word carry while glancing across her shoulder in the direction of the television. When she turned back to Laura, the woman was finally gazing fixedly at the screen.

Laura looked to Tielle. "Yuck."

Tielle's smile was grim. "You catch my meaning?"

"Loud and clear." Laura tapped her index finger against her cheek as she considered the mounting issue. "We need something to mix things up, you think?"

"Not necessarily." Tielle leaned on the credenza and worried the end of the French braid she'd used to tame her coarse, lengthy hair that day. "All we really need is a break between sessions. Give the weather a chance to stabilize and if it gets the better of us—" she shrugged her shoulders "—at least we tried."

Laura scrunched her nose. "I don't know, Ti…that's a lot of time to be off the clock. We usually close down for the holidays well into New Year's. Do we really want to do more than that?"

"We've had a good year." Tielle cleared her throat when her heart suddenly seized over what, for her at least, was a lie.

"Ah, Ti, I'm sorry." Laura had easily sensed the change in her boss's mood. "It's the anniversary, isn't it?" She closed her eyes while her palm went to slap her forehead over the gaffe.

Tielle's round, pretty face had recaptured a measure of control. "Not quite an anniversary."

"Have you talked to him?" Laura's voice sounded hushed.

Tielle looked to the fall foliage beyond the window. "Not since the day we signed the papers." She thought about crossing the room to take a closer look at the view but reconsidered when a light sheen of tears blurred her gaze.

"Still too soon to think about it all?" Laura guessed.

"Still too soon." Tielle's reply was monotone.

Laura turned back to the projected calendar. "That's what I told him." Her words were faint, absently delivered.

Still, they were amplified enough to catch Tielle's ears. "Told who?"

"You had a call last week from Faro Clegg."

Silent, Tielle returned to sit behind her wide walnut desk where she repeated the name of her ex-brother-in-law in her mind. It was a name she'd not allowed herself to think of since she'd signed her divorce papers one year ago that day.

"What'd he want?" she finally asked her assistant, her voice still harboring the same monotone.

"We didn't cover many details." Laura watched her booted foot swing idly back and forth. "The gist of the call was about him wanting to talk to you about arranging a weeklong stay."

"For Clegg Marketing?"

Laura looked uncomfortable, her booted foot swinging a bit more vivaciously. "For the Clegg family."

Portland, Oregon

"Is this fact or gossip?"

The voice coasting from behind the massive walled bar space instilled a spine-tapping tingle beneath Leonard Cartright's skin. Nevertheless, as he'd already come to the table with his suspicions, he knew it'd be pointless to play the cautious role then.

"What I just told you was hearsay." Despite his resolve, Leonard exercised care in handling what he knew to be a highly sensitive issue.

"I.e., gossip."

Leonard cringed. "*Gossip* has got such an ugly ring to it."

"Mmm…and yet I keep on hearing it." Graedon Clegg's movements could easily be described by any variation or synonym of the word *sleek*. Artful, really, given his striking build, easily mesmerizing when partnered with other attributes.

Graedon moved from behind the bar and passed a drink to his late father's oldest friend. "Calm down, Leo," he urged.

Leo Cartright didn't care if the man he reported to was a kid beneath him. Only a fool would come to deliver unsavory news to Graedon Clegg and be on anything other than heightened alert. This stood whether Graedon was offering a drink or a challenge to a brawl.

"Come on, Leo, I need you to talk to me here." Grae allowed his concern to show, hoping it'd urge Leo to speak freely. Grae let his uncle in name only glimpse his concern and hoped it'd urge the man to speak freely. Anticipating the moods of his associates was one of the things that made him such a formidable opponent at work and play.

Leo downed a bit of the gin and tonic he'd requested. "Working for your brother's become too volatile," he admitted once a few sips of the crisp drink had bubbled on his tongue.

"In what way?" Grae appeared the image of maddening cool as he eased behind the no-nonsense blackwood desk in the stark corner office.

Leo's jaw dropped, his eyes growing wide.

Graedon shrugged, a smile narrowing an unexpected bronze stare. "Humor me," he urged, his palm stroking the sleek stubble shading his jaw and adding something rugged to an otherwise pretty face.

"Something's got him…changed. Something subtle but it's strong. I don't know…" Leo reached for the drink, downed another hearty swig. "He's still the same ol' Faro—dictating, strutting around like a little Napoleon."

Grae let slip a soft chuckle as the image of his older brother came to mind. Leo had captured Faro Clegg perfectly.

"Sorry," Leo said, yet the grin remained on his attractive, dark face.

"So what's changed?" Grae asked.

"Well…" Leo expelled a perplexed sigh. "He's still got the little-big-man complex, but it's like he's not as…I don't know…pressured by all of it as he used to be. Hell if I know, Grae…" Leo leaned back in the deep armchair he occupied and smoothed a hand across the soft salt-and-pepper hair tapered at his nape. "It's like he's got the skinny on somethin' the rest of us don't. I don't want to find myself on the evil side of his bad personality if what he knows is that I've been feeding you info on how he's running his side of the business."

Grae leaned forward a bit in his own chair. "Are you trying to tell me you confirmed the suspicions you came to me with last month—ones in addition to what you gave me six months ago?"

"What can I say? Your brother is one long, consistent train wreck, but this part is still hearsay."

"Hearsay," Grae groaned. He angled his gaze toward the low file cabinet that ran the length of the rear wall when the phone there buzzed. He ignored the sound. "Anybody willing to name names? Names bold enough not to hide behind the gossip, but to defend their words."

Leo didn't seem hopeful. "Come on, Grae, nobody wants to brush up against Faro, especially when it could mean getting caught between something with you on the other side of it. Everyone knows what a fierce position that could be," he muttered, rolling his eyes.

The phone buzzed again. Grae answered, primarily to get thoughts best left alone to venture out of his mind.

Leo took advantage of the break in conversation to enjoy the rest of his drink. He'd finished it off before Grae's rich rumble of a voice became a veritable rasp as he next addressed the unfortunate soul on the other end of the phone line. When he apologized to the caller, Leo realized he was talking to his assistant, Emily Claude.

"I don't need to see it, Em. Hold on to it till I get out there, all right?" Grae set the phone to its receiver, studied it for an extended moment. "What do you know about a retreat?" he asked before swiveling his desk chair back to face Leo.

"Somethin' to do with Faro?" Leo asked.

"No idea." Grae stood, rounded his desk and went to refill the drink for the man who was more like a brother to him than his own. "Sounds like he's trying to put together some kind of retreat for the family."

Leo watched Grae slosh more gin into their stout glasses. Silently, he considered the event. Family retreats and reunions usually had the makings of a lot of unnecessary drama. "Is that it?" He reclaimed the glass Grae handed over. "A retreat made you scare Em that way?"

"He's already handing out invites to the damn thing." Grae set aside his drink and went about rolling the sleeves of a navy shirt over wide forearms corded with muscle. "Dropped mine off a few minutes ago. It's waiting on Em's desk. Location? Turner Estates and Gardens."

"Lord." Leo slumped down into his chair. "Is it confirmed? The place? I just can't imagine—" Leo paused over speaking Tielle's name. He knew that wound was still raw, too fresh, even for Graedon to hear without being affected.

Grae needed no additional clarification at any rate. "Em says there's an asterisk next to the location name designating that it's 'subject to change,' so…"

"You think it will?"

Grae shrugged off Leo's soft inquiry. "Doesn't matter. I'm not going anyway." Out of frustrated habit he fingered the dark curls that covered his head in a halo of glossy black.

Leo didn't bother disputing the comment. He wondered if Grae heard the doubt in his voice as clearly as *he* did. "Why do you think he's organizing a lovefest for the family?" he asked instead.

"Besides the fact that we could really use one?" Grae smirked.

It was relatively true. While a measure of goodwill existed among the various cliques within the Clegg family, overall, there was still a measure of bad blood that could at any time erupt into a smelly mess. Such problems among the Clegg brood had been well covered over the decades, ever since Kenneth Clegg's advertisements for African-American products and businesses began to appear in national magazines.

Faro and Graedon Clegg's father had continued to outdo himself. The man's accomplishments had boosted Clegg Marketing from one plateau to another. Sadly, Ken

Clegg's successes were matched all too greatly by the dramas in his personal life. Most unfortunate was the fact that the greatest portion of that drama originated in his family.

Nevertheless, Ken's bright spot had been Clegg Marketing—his baby, his brain child. The visionary had even welcomed his family to share in what gave him such joy. The man's heart was as big and robust as the man had been himself. When he died, family, friends and business rivals alike had all mourned his passing.

Yet when Graedon Clegg assumed the role as CEO of the company, few argued the virtually unarguable; Ken Clegg's tenacious persona and dogged work ethic tempered by compassion and good humor seemed to have been reborn in his youngest son.

"Maybe Faro's motivations for this retreat have something to do with your gossip." Grae finished rolling his sleeves and reached for his drink.

A bark of laughter leaped from Leo's heavyset frame. "It's rumored that your brother might be ready to jump a ship he set ablaze and leave a ruined kingdom in your capable hands, and you think he'd throw a party at some ritzy resort to celebrate?"

"The place isn't a resort," Grae muttered into his glass before drinking from it. "Do you really think he'd do that ever? Leave? Leave it all to me, besides? 'Cause I sure as hell don't."

Leo shook his head.

"There're often faint orbs of truth in rumors," Grae said. "Whatever Faro's doing isn't being done in preparation for Faro leaving, but for *me* leaving."

Leo barked another laugh. "But that's crazy! He'd

be a fool to think anyone would side with him to make that happen."

That much was also true. At thirty-six, Grae had secured his place at the helm of his family. It wasn't predestined. Most of the Clegg family had believed they'd had the next great football superstar instead of the next powerhouse ad exec. He was massively built and athletically talented to boot, so it was a logical assumption. Alas, Grae had inherited his father's business savvy and passion for the ad game, as well.

Regrettably, the prodigy Ken Clegg had found in his youngest son wasn't a hit with everyone in the Clegg family. Faro wasn't of a mind to relinquish his birthright to his baby brother, no matter how much natural talent the man had.

It was of little consequence, however, given the fact that the rest of the Clegg family believed that Grae had what it took to make Ken Clegg's legacy flourish and keep them all on the positive side of wealth for the foreseeable future. When the board of Clegg Marketing unanimously decided to place Grae in the top seat, many thought Faro would be too humiliated to remain— including Grae, who had been as surprised as anyone when his brother had chosen to stay aboard.

Unlike the rest of the family, who figured that Faro had come around to the majority's way of thinking, Grae had a different feeling entirely regarding his brother's motives. He believed the man was just biding his time, waiting for Grae to royally screw up or to throw in the towel.

Grae knew that a year ago that day, Faro had almost gotten his wish.

"So what now?" Leo asked. "Are you going to try and

find out what he's up to this time or just wait and let the chips fall where they may?"

"There's an invitation out there with my name on it." Grae rolled back one shoulder in a lazy shrug. "Chips will probably fall anyway."

"And what about that invite?" Leo balanced his emptied glass on the perfect crease of one black trouser leg. "The venue? You gonna put a stop to that?" Leo frowned in a playfully curious manner when Grae responded to his question with a slow smile.

Tielle was halfway to the midmorning breakfast meeting she had only ten more minutes to get to when she realized she'd forgotten the presentation she'd prepared for the counseling center that was scouting Turner Estates for an upcoming summer retreat. Her brain had been so mushy by the time she'd left the office the day before that she had totally forgotten it. It was what she got for spending such late nights at the office instead of going home like a regular woman.

Her thoughts drifted as she edited her silent realization. All the *regular women* she knew had reasons to go home—family, a husband or special man… Until little over a year ago, she'd had that. She could say that losing Grae had hit her out of nowhere, but that wasn't true.

She'd seen their issues turning into more serious problems down the road. She'd done nothing to stop them, but he'd given her every chance to, hadn't he?

He'd given you his…ultimatum—

Tielle shook off the thoughts. She didn't need them that day, not when business called so strongly. Mind refocused on the presentation, Tielle barely shut the door before she parked the car in the grand horseshoe drive before the main house.

Dashing inside, she was taking the various corridors toward the administrative offices when her mobile hummed. She fished the phone from her bag, answering as she rounded another corridor.

"Good morning, this is Tielle."

"Well, Tielle, I must say it's good to hear you sounding so chipper."

The trail Tielle blazed to her office came to an abrupt stop on the blocky heels of her chic boots. "Faro," she said, hearing her ex-brother-in-law chuckle over the surprise in her voice.

"Sorry for jumping the gun and not waiting on you to return my call, sweetness, but you know I've never been the patient sort."

"I remember." Slowly, Tielle put her feet in motion, resuming the journey to her office. "And I haven't made a decision about your event. but I'm leaning toward a 'no.' I don't think it's a good idea, and *you know*—" she turned his words around on him "—half your family can't even stand me."

"But your place is the best, Tielle."

"Lots of places are just as good."

"I need the group in high spirits and they have such… happy memories of your place."

Tielle forced more life into her feet, lest she settle to the floor right there in the middle of the corridor. Faro's mention of "happy times" at Turner Estates promised to do just that.

"Listen, Faro, I appreciate the nudge and the business, but I really can't spare time to talk about this now. I, um—I'm on my way to a meeting." She sighed, pulling steel into her voice. "Now would you rather a slow yes or a fast no?"

Tielle listened for a response, only hearing Faro take his turn at sighing. Her thumb hovered over the end button on the mobile, prepared to shut down the call.

"Guess I have to wait. This means a lot to me, Tielle." His authoritative voice drifted through the line then.

"The wait won't be long." Tielle rolled her eyes, silently criticizing her need to offer reassurance, especially to Faro Clegg. "But I'm swamped right now, so it won't be today."

"Yes, yes of course, Tielle, and thank you. I hope you'll accept my apologies for my impatience and insensitivity."

Once again, Tielle's steps slowed. "Insensitivity?"

"Wasn't it today? Or sometime this week that you signed the papers to divorce Grae?" Faro's voice sounded heavier, stressed. "I'll always hold myself to blame for that, Ti."

"Thanks, um, I really do need to be going." The present topic was one Tielle was certainly in no state to discuss, and especially not with the man on the other end of her line. "I appreciate your concern..." She quickened her pace en route to the office.

"Certainly, Tielle, I'll let you get on with your day."

Tielle pressed the end button without further ceremony. She rushed past the beveled glass doors leading into Turner Estates's administrative wing. The hem of the blue-gray dress she wore flipped with more intensity with the somewhat frantic nature of her pace. Faro's call had her more agitated than she wanted to admit.

"Morning!" She tossed a blanket greeting over the

room, not bothering to make eye contact with her staff or any waiting visitors.

"I only need to grab the rest of the counseling center presentation," she told Laura on her way past where the woman stood speaking with her assistant, Marisol Estes.

Tielle slammed her office door, effectively silencing what Laura was calling out to her just then.

Finding the storyboard mock-ups where she'd expected them was enough to improve Tielle's mood a bit from Faro's unexpected call…and the apology that followed. She was giving the presentation a final thumb-through when a single knock sounded on the door.

"Sorry, Laura. I just needed to grab this. I'm already crazy late…" Eyes still focused on the portfolio, Tielle opened the door, waiting for Laura to walk in with conversation.

There was only silence, which eventually drew her gaze. The portfolio slipped from her fingers when she discovered that the knock hadn't come from her colleague but her husband.

Ex.

Graedon Clegg filled the doorway with shoulders that threatened to brush the frame.

"Spare a little time for me, Tel," he said.

Chapter 2

He didn't give her the option to accept or decline. Of course he wouldn't. Any man who had to angle sideways to clear a doorway didn't wait for permission to enter any room. When he knelt before her instead of entering, though, Tielle jumped as if she'd been scorched.

Grae bent to retrieve the portfolio Tielle had dropped. He offered her the folder, smiling so slightly that it may've been missed when she didn't reach to take it.

Grae hung on to the portfolio, using it as an added excuse to move deeper into the office. There, he set the presentation on the desk and took a seat on its edge.

"Close the door."

He was *asking* if she would close the door. Again, there was rarely another answer besides yes when Graedon Clegg asked a question. Tielle had always considered it an annoying habit. That was before time in her husband's—*ex*-husband's—presence had clued her into the fact that it was purposefully done. He asked questions in such a manner that to respond in the negative seemed strange.

Close the door. Spare a little time for me, Tel.

Tielle closed the door, leaning back against it in hopes that her stance would seem easy as opposed to wilting.

"You're a little early, aren't you?" She forced herself to speak with the same ease she was hoping to perpetuate in her stance.

"Meaning?" He smiled at her query.

"I haven't even given an answer yet."

"Answer." He frowned. "Answer for what?"

Tielle pushed off the door, not completely closing the distance between them but moving just close enough for her to study his expression.

Good one, Ti, she silently admonished herself.

Studying Grae Clegg's expression was only a sidebar to the real intent, which was just…studying. Marveling, actually, over the combination of features that created a divinely constructed face. She blinked, having caught the faint smile that he was never quite fast enough to hide from her. He revealed it whenever he knew he had achieved whatever it was that he sought.

"I told your brother I needed time to think on it." Tielle coolly added distance between them, moving behind her desk. "But I told Faro I didn't think it was a good idea." She didn't sit, merely stood tapping her fingers to the semicluttered surface of the desk.

"Tel." Grae spread his hands in sync with his grin while pretending to come clean. "I got no idea what you're talking about."

"That's impossible." Suspicion clouded the clear cognac hue of her eyes. "You know every move he makes."

"That was only when he tried to make them with you."

She bristled. "He never tried to make them with me."

"You never realized it."

"Which brings us back to why it's impossible for you not to know what he's up to."

"Not exactly." Grae smoothed the back of his hand

across the dark shadow of whiskers on his cheek. "The moves you make are no longer any of my business, are they?"

The outright question put Tielle in her seat, yet she managed to make the move appear graceful enough.

"Faro says he wants to book the estate exclusively for one week. He wants to hold a Clegg family retreat." She shared the explanation politely enough. Admirably, she subdued the wound his words had opened. She wanted to maintain eye contact. Sadly, all she could focus on, as Grae sat there stroking his jaw, was his sleek beard, which added an intimidation factor and needed no additional emphasis.

Those inky whiskers contrasted so richly against an otherwise flawless palette of light caramel. They felt like mink against her skin when he kissed her...wherever he kissed her—used to kiss her...

"He told you *what* prompted such a great idea?" he asked.

"Well, I don't know, Grae. Maybe he thinks he can fix your family." With a laugh, she stood and left the desk. Silently, she reiterated the conversation she'd just had with Faro. "I'm pretty sure a fast no is the right answer here. Listen, Grae, I have a meeting I'm already late for." Hastily, she rounded the desk and began collecting her things.

Grae was blocking her way before Tielle even moved from the desk, causing her to swallow around her heart in her throat.

"I'd like for you not to do that, Tel."

The urgency in the canyon depth of his voice gave Tielle pause. "Tell me why?" It was her chance to mask command in the form of a question.

Grae clenched his jaw, revealing the defeat he felt. "I honestly don't know, Tel, but going through with this thing might bring it all out."

Tielle dismissed the voice warning her not to ask and asked anyway. "Can't Faro want to retreat for exactly what retreats are meant for? To fix things?"

Graedon smiled, but the gesture held no humor and very little softness. "Still blind when it comes to my brother," he accused.

"So are you." She smiled and shrugged. "I guess we're a perfect pair then."

"We used to be." A more pronounced element filtered the bronze of his stare.

"Is it refusal or acceptance you want, Grae?"

When he smiled, Tielle wondered if he was confused about what she should have been refusing or accepting.

"Acceptance."

Confusion crept in on her then. He was frowning in that way he did when seeking to relay the importance of what he was saying. Tielle refused to get lost in his very capable ability to spellbind her.

"Why would you want me to accept Faro's request? Wouldn't that make him a little too happy?"

"May be the only way to get to the bottom of what he's really up to."

"Grae..." Tielle rubbed at the bridge of her nose. "What does all this suspicion get you?"

"Not nearly as much as it's lost me."

"And yet you continue to pursue it."

His jaw clenched again. "I pursue it so that I can crush it."

A soft spurt of laughter rippled past her lips.

"What?" His eyes raked the length of her, focusing on Tielle's bottom when she turned away.

She set her meeting materials back on the desk. "Just that your…pursuit might be self-defeating, is all."

"Okay," Grae prompted.

"*It* didn't lose you anything. *You* did."

Grae bowed his head and shook it as though he wasn't surprised by her point of view. "He's not what you think, Tel. He never has been."

"It must be so sad to live your life only seeing the worst in everyone."

"Not everyone, Tel. Just him."

When she turned away with a submissive sigh, Grae came down off some of his anger. "Tel—"

"Don't, okay? The quicker all this gets started, the quicker I get all of you out of my hair." She distanced herself again. "I'll give Faro a call after my meeting…"

Grae was barely listening. The reference she'd made to her hair had his eyes fixed upon the fluffy mass. Coarse-textured and flowing, it framed her round face like an enchanting dark cloud. He knew she usually tamed the wild tresses into a thick ball, only leaving it wild about her face when she was heading out for the evening or going to bed…

Who did she say she was meeting again? he wondered.

Something to do with business, but it mattered little. Tielle could capture a man's eyes and stir his appraisal— no matter the venue. Her curvy proportions, untamed hair and baby-doll allure had anchored him with an invisible yet irresistible hook since the day he'd met her.

He was still anchored to her. Of course he was, with only his anger and suspicion to hold on to. She was right—what he'd lost, it was all on him.

"Grae?" Tielle waited until he'd focused on her. "Is that it?"

He watched her so meaningfully in that moment that Tielle was forced to glance down at her dress to see if it was still clinging to her body.

"For now." He pushed off the arm of the chair. "Thanks, Tel."

She managed to stay on her feet until he'd pulled the door shut behind him.

"I'm so sorry, Ti." Laura offered her apology while adding more of the ginger dressing to her salad. "He was already here when I got in this morning." Done with the dressing, she blew at a tuft of her bobbed hair. "And we must not forget our helpful man-crazy staff. They'd already given him your full itinerary for the day."

"Our man-crazy staff?" Tielle gave Laura a look of mock reproach. "Are you trying to suddenly distance yourself from the bunch?"

"Well, hell, Ti, I mean, can you blame us?" Laura was crunching around a mouthful of salad by then. "Especially when it's Graedon Clegg who comes a-callin'? What woman wouldn't drop everything to…help him?" She closed her eyes over her word selection and winced. "Sorry."

"No…" Tielle was giggling a mite helplessly. "I need the laugh."

"So?" Laura pretended to be focused on the wide salad bowl she clutched. "You gonna tell me what happened in there? Every woman out here was falling all over the man when he got here. He was polite enough." She shrugged beneath the lime-green cropped neck sweater she wore. "He really was pretty sweet, but he didn't really come alive until you walked in. You were ranting so...didn't even notice him following you to your office like you were dragging him along with a leash. Humph...pretty amazing to watch."

It was pretty amazing to hear, and Tielle listened to the recap in awe.

"It's been a year and I still can't quite wrap my head around what happened." A shiver touched her arm, and she began a slow rub to rush warmth to the limb. "We loved each other—wanted each other *all* the time." Tielle let her lashes drift downward and swallowed with effort as emotion promised to close her throat while memories set her arousal mounting. She shook her head in a poor attempt to ward them off.

"What went wrong between us didn't have to." She looked out at the sunny environment beyond the long windows running past the tables in the staff cafeteria where she and Laura had their lunch.

"I'm sorry, Ti. It—it's none of my business."

"It's okay." Tielle leaned over to warm her fingertips against her teacup. "Maybe talking about it will help. Nothing else does." She looked at Laura squarely then. "Grae wanted me to stop talking to his brother and I wouldn't. I thought I could fix whatever was wrong between them." She considered the shade of the blueberry tea then. "I didn't know how impossible that was until I lost him—until I lost my husband. It's not like I didn't see it coming, but helping people find their way back to one another is what I'm supposed to be best at, right?"

Laura replied with a sympathetic smile. Yes, if anyone had a knack for fixing things between people, it was Tielle Turner. She got it honest. It was, after all, in her blood.

Named for her grandmothers, Tina and Danielle, Tielle had continued the women's legacy for helping mend relationship fences. Tielle had never met a lost cause she turned away from. She had continually found great success in helping people—families, especially, through their trials.

That was before she'd taken on the task of trying to fix what was broken between her ex-husband and his brother.

"He wanted you to go against who you are," Laura noted.

Sighing, Tielle raised her brows in a resigned fashion. "I'm just as much at fault. I should've left it alone…at the very least I should've suggested that they talk with someone else, and then I should've just let it go."

"But what was wrong was hurting him, and that's hard to turn away from," Laura argued gently.

Tielle finally gave attention to the chef salad she'd ordered. "*I* thought it was hurting him—" she sprinkled on pepper "—but it was just the way things were between them. The way they'd always been. No need to be fixed—Grae had accepted it long ago and had accepted it so much that I didn't get how serious he was when he told me to leave it alone or we were done."

Laura munched through her salad for a time and then looked up at Tielle. "Do you think he'll come to the retreat if it all goes through?"

"Sounded like he was fishing for something…" Tielle's voice had a faint introspective quality. "He'd need to be here to get what he's after, right?"

"And what does that mean for you?"

"You know I never stay around for the retreats." Tielle favored Laura with a wink. "That's what I pay my team of savvy fixers to do."

"But aren't you curious?" Laura's voice was hushed.

"I'm not even a *little* curious." Tielle gestured as though she were wiping her hands. "I plan to call Faro, hash out the details for the event and then get the hell out of here before the first Clegg arrives."

"And what'll you do if you're one of the Cleggs he wants here?"

Tielle only hesitated momentarily before saying, "I'm not a Clegg anymore."

"Because of him," Laura reminded. "What if he wants to fix what he broke between you and Grae?"

"Faro didn't break anything, Laura." Tielle shook her head defiantly. "The prize for all that goes to me and my ex-husband."

Though the decision was already made, Tielle gave herself a couple of days more before making things official with Faro. His unexpected call the week before had better prepared her to hear his voice when his assistant patched him through. Yet memories stirred of the good and bad times comprising her old life and made getting through the call more of a chore than was expected.

"My assistant, Laura Cooper, will be your facilitator for the event. We'll be forwarding an information packet for you to review and sign," she said as the call rounded out. "You can give her a call with any questions."

"And can you be reached at this number, or is your cell still the best?"

"No, they're both fine, but you won't need to talk to me since Laura will be handling it all."

"Smart move. That way you'll have the chance to enjoy the retreat as a guest."

"Guest?" Tielle stopped the idle tap of a pump-shod

foot against the bottom drawer of her desk. "Faro, I'm no longer involved once the initial organization of the event is handled. I never take part in the retreats—least of all as a guest."

"Understood. But I will need you to make a special exception in this case."

"Faro...I—"

"This is your family, too."

"Faro, not even when I was married to Grae. It was never my family."

"Don't you think it's time to change that?" he challenged.

Tielle puffed out her cheeks, her taps to the bottom desk drawer gaining force. "Faro, considering the fact that your brother and I are divorced—"

"For only a year."

"Divorced is divorced."

"He still loves you, Ti."

"Don't do this, Faro. It's long past time. I'm as done with this as Grae is."

"Humph. Well, Ti, that'd mean you aren't done at all. Honey, Grae...well, he's changed a lot since he lost you." Faro's sigh carried on a defeated breath. "That... bad side that people hope they never see, much less have directed their way, is pretty much all they have to work with these days."

"That's got nothing to do with me." Tielle gave a nervous tug to the end of her low ponytail. "That *bad side* is pretty much all I saw toward the end and that was *before* he lost me, Faro."

"He lost you because of me—"

"Faro—"

"That kind heart of yours won't let you admit that,

but you know it's true. I need to fix things with you as much as I do with my blood relatives."

"Faro, listen to me." She kept her tone measured as though she were speaking to a recalcitrant child. "I have no anger that I'm holding on to toward you. I need you to accept that."

"All right, Tielle, all right. But I need honest emotion from everyone. I won't get that from Grae unless you're there."

"So Grae *is* coming?" Tielle tried to sound airy, but merely came off as nonplussed.

"I'm still working on it, but my chances would be better at encouraging him if you—"

"I don't want to play those games, Faro."

"Tielle, *I* need you guys there if I plan to start mending those fences. That's all. I'd think you of all people could appreciate that."

Tielle pushed out of her chair and gave the air a frustrated kick when she stepped from behind her desk.

"Ti?" Faro called when long silence had held the line.

"I'll do my best to be there and that's the best answer I can give you right now."

"Understood." Faro sounded as though her words translated into a flat yes to his request.

Tielle heard the glee loud and clear, but she had no energy to stifle it then. "Goodbye, Faro." She disconnected without waiting for a farewell from his end.

Back in Portland, Oregon, Faro Clegg's smile mirrored his inner glee. That emotion, however, was short-lived when a knock hit the door and his brother walked into the office without waiting on permission to enter.

"Got all your RSVPs in place?" Grae asked, giving Faro's desk an assessing bronzed stare.

"As usual, I don't know what the hell you're talking about."

"Right." Grae waved the invite to the retreat he'd received and watched Faro's tired smirk transform to one of knowing.

"All RSVPs received, but one," Faro admitted, nodding toward the one his brother waved. "Thanks for coming to reply in person."

"Tell me more about it," Grae urged.

Faro pushed his chair back a little from his desk. "Just a family get-together. Thought we could use it, and who better than the two biggest troublemakers to set it all in motion?"

"So you expect me to be there, why? Because of Tielle?"

"I thought she'd be the best motivator, yes, but no one, no *place* is better at giving folks what they need to fix their issues than Tielle and her people there."

"Is she helping you with this?" Grae's voice had taken on a leaden quality. One that sent more menace into his bottomless voice.

"No." Again, honesty shone in Faro's dark face. "I'll be lucky if I can even get her to stick around for it."

Grae's stirring eyes fell to the invite. "Did she say she wouldn't?"

Faro scooted his chair back toward the desk and made a pretense of shuffling papers there. "I think she'll try."

A glimmer of intrigue sharpened Grae's expression when he regarded the invite again.

"So? Do you think you'll try to make it?" Faro was still feigning interest in the contents of his desk.

"Don't try to con me, Faro." Grae's steely demeanor instantly redefined itself.

"It's no con." Faro reared back in his chair and made eye contact with his brother. "I only want the family strong—united."

"Why?"

"Because we're family!"

"Bullshit." A muscle flexed devilishly along Grae's jaw so powerfully that the movement was visible beneath the sleek whiskers shading his face. "Tielle isn't family."

"Please, Grae, you haven't believed that since you let her go."

Graedon pushed a hand into the pocket of his dark trousers in order to hide a fist he'd clenched. "You want to fix our family yet you pick my ex-wife's place as the venue to do it?"

"Ex-wife? Is that what she is to you?" Faro smiled when Grae staggered back. Quickly, he moved from his desk and left his brother alone in the office.

Chapter 3

Located just outside Vancouver, Turner Estates and Gardens was a remote spread of property that had once been a successful dairy farm until the farm's owners decided to live out their days relaxing instead of working.

When Avery Turner and his wife, Danielle, proposed purchasing the farm from the elderly growers, there was, of course, great concern. The Turners, after all, were a young black couple, and such business arrangements, especially in those days, were rare. Still, the aged farmers obviously saw something they liked in the couple, for they ordered their sons to sell to Avery Turner and give him what he needed to succeed.

What Avery needed most was his best friend, Lucas Mayes. When Lucas arrived with his wife, Tina, in tow, the foursome ran the farm in a manner no one could fault. The couples eventually decided to sell off the cattle and make their profit opening the breathtaking and expansive gardens to tourists.

Vancouver and neighboring Victoria were often visited by artists, musicians and hosts of academics. Such venues as the Turner and Mayes Gardens were especially popular. In later years, wedding bells resounded between the Turners' son, Aaron, and the Mayeses' Vanessa. The older generation entrusted their life's work to the new, and Turner Estates and Gardens was born.

When both Avery Turner and Lucas Mayes passed on, their wives embarked on a new venture—inviting small groups to meditate in the gardens for extended periods. During that time, Tina Mayes and Danielle Turner held time for fellowship and scripture reading. The women found they had a love for it upon witnessing the transformation it made among their guests.

When the family business fell to her to control, Tielle decided to move things to a larger scale. Turner Estates and Gardens became an exclusive retreat for families, executives, social groups…the list was long, diverse and distinguished. Tielle's therapists were respected for their abilities as well as their discretion.

The business venture had been a smart and lucrative one. Tielle had never regretted continuing what her grandmothers had started. During the last year, however, the picture perfection of her business had shown signs of wear around the edges. Every room, every tree or garden path, it seemed, held a memory that reminded her of Graedon Clegg.

They'd been married there. Spent part of their honeymoon there. The place had always been a magical one for her. In spite of what had happened between her and Grae, it was still a magical place. Nevertheless, memories definitely took their toll.

How was she to function when the most potent aspect of those memories was there in the flesh? Faro could forget it, she decided. Tielle stared out from the corner of her office that looked toward the hill that led in from the dirt road and would transport guests on or off the property. The Clegg clan would be arriving at any time. What to do, what to do…

"Still time to make a run for it…" Laura must have been reading Tielle's mind when she arrived in the office singing the possibility.

"Don't think it hasn't occurred to me…" Tielle sang back, toying with the paisley-print tie of her wrap shirt.

"You don't have to do anything you don't want to, you know."

Tielle puffed out a thoughtful breath. "I know that, too…"

"Meaning?"

"Meaning…" Tielle turned to sit on the windowsill. "I'm out of here the minute those people have visions of gumdrops dancing in their sleepy heads."

Laura leaned against the doorjamb, folded her arms over her middle. "What about Grae?"

"Humph." Tielle leaned back against the window. "I doubt he'll miss me."

Silently, she recalled what he'd said about her not being his business anymore. Looking out the window again, she noticed two SUVs coming down the hill and leaving clouds of dust in their wake.

She smiled. "And the drama begins."

Laura joined Tielle at the window to observe the procession. "Why don't you let *me* greet the gang? *You* can receive your guests in the sunroom."

Tielle squeezed the hand Laura had clasped over her forearm. "Thanks, girl."

A serious look stole across Laura's honey-toned face. "You don't owe these people anything."

With that reminder, Laura left the office.

Alone, Tielle turned her gaze beyond the window,

watching as the two SUVs drew closer to the main house. Several yards behind them were a trio of cars.

Yes, she thought, the gang was all here.

She was sure none of *the gang* would want to miss out on the chance to tell her what they thought of her. Not that they hadn't made a career of doing so during her marriage to Grae. Tielle rolled her eyes as more vehicles traversed the dirt road leading in.

Resolute, she stood and walked across the office to give herself a once-over in the floor-length mirror on the door to her private bathroom. Satisfied, she set out.

Tielle was certain that Faro would want to make an entrance and bask in the accomplishment of bringing his family together under one roof for the purpose of healing. Instead, he walked in among the group laughing and talking as if his family's close bonds had never been tested and that *he* hadn't been the one who had tested them the most.

Laura must have told Faro where to find Tielle. He was first to arrive in the sunroom that faced the enormous and professionally manicured rear lawn.

"Ti!" The short, dark man greeted his ex-sister-in-law with open arms. "Thanks for agreeing to this," he said while squeezing her in his welcome embrace.

"Faro, I—"

"Well, well, isn't this a familiar sight? The two best buds cozied up."

The unmistakable female voice reached Tielle's ears before she could complete her response to Faro. She looked around the man's slender frame to see his cousins Ranata and Asia. It was Asia who had spoken. The statuesque lovely sauntered into the sunroom. Her stiletto boots intermittently clicked and quieted as they moved from the hardwood flooring to the plush, ornately designed throws in the expansive room. She took inventory of the breathtaking spot as though there was little truly impressive about the area.

Late-afternoon sunlight was beginning to cascade into the room, sending spectrums of color through the cut-glass lamp bottoms and bathing the healthy potted plants and deep, cushioned furnishings in liquid gold.

"Another expensive retreat on the books, Ti-Ti?" Asia's voice was husky yet with a distinctly nasal element. "Aren't you already getting enough of Grae's money in the settlement?"

"Nice to see you, Asia," Tielle somehow managed.

Asia's glossy, full lips twisted into a nasty smile. "No need to lie."

"All right, then." Tielle tried not to appear too gleeful when Asia's smile froze.

"Sorry to interrupt." Laura arrived then with two of the retreat's baggage attendants in tow. "We're about to take a look at the sleeping quarters, if you all would be so kind as to join us?"

Asia had recovered somewhat from her embarrassment. "Come on, Ranata," she ordered the silent, petite woman at her side.

Faro looked apologetic and rubbed Tielle's shoulder when the women had gone. "I know this won't be easy," he said.

"Smart man."

Faro grinned. "I *am* thankful that you agreed to all this."

Tielle folded her arms. "Looks like Grae didn't accept your invite. Maybe you won't need me here for this after all."

"Mr. Clegg?" Laura called to Faro before he could respond to Tielle. "Would you mind joining the others for a moment?"

Tielle caught Laura's eye with a glance of gratitude when Faro obliged without comment. Alone in the dazzling room, Tielle hid her face behind her palms and groaned. Once her emotions began to settle, she went back to the windows to take stock of the cars lining the yard and prepared herself for the next round of guests.

Tielle had thrown herself into taking care of busywork for most of the afternoon. Following the *warm* reunion with Asia and Ranata, Tielle was better prepared for the rest of her ex's chilly female cousins. She received even less warmth from the older Clegg women and had taken to checking her watch often in hopes of finding that dinner was served or that the much anticipated bedtime had arrived.

She'd stopped off to check on things in the kitchen—a place that usually soothed frazzled nerves. Especially true now, because she saw works of edible art being created when she arrived. That evening, the cook staff was in their element and ready to boast about their efforts. They offered Tielle samples of what they had planned for the evening's meal.

The plate of spinach and cream cheese pinwheels, bourbon and scallion chicken strips and vegetable sautéed rice put a small but welcomed coating on Tielle's stomach. The treat gave her the strength—she hoped—to handle the remainder of her hellacious evening.

"That was fantastic, guys! Can't wait for dinner!" Tielle was in high spirits as she took the kitchen exit. In the corridor, she ran into an unexpected guest.

Laughing as much from relief as happiness, Tielle fell into the open arms of yet another Clegg family member. She greeted Desree Clegg, the eldest of the Clegg family and Ken Clegg's sister.

"What are you doing here in all this madness?" Happier than she'd been in a long time, Tielle pressed a kiss to the woman's cheek.

Desree Clegg's plump caramel-toned face was even lovelier than usual thanks to the brightness of her smile. "I could ask the same of you, miss," she scolded.

"Faro asked me to stay."

The explanation dimmed Des's smile a little. "What's that boy up to?"

Tielle laughed. "You sound just like Grae." Instantly, she regretted the slip when a knowing light crept into Desree's dark eyes.

"Is that a…recent insight?"

"Des…I've only seen him once and that was only so he could ask me to go along with Faro having the retreat here."

Desree snorted. "Now what's *that* boy up to?"

Tielle linked an arm through the crook of Desree's. "Maybe they're finally trying to come together."

Rich laughter tumbled from a still shapely mouth when Des threw back her head. "The only thing those two have ever come together over is *nothing*."

Tielle laughed again, feeling ever more peaceful in the presence of her favorite Clegg.

"You know you don't need to be here." Desree's reminder held a warning.

"I'm jumping ship as soon as everyone's safely tucked away in their beds."

"And what will you do if Grae personally asks you to stay?"

"Is he coming?" Tielle felt as though lead was weighing her down and keeping her pinned to her spot.

"It makes sense, doesn't it?" Desree's dark eyes sparkled as vibrantly as the small row of sequins lining the pocket of her lavender smock blouse. "I mean, he *did* make a point of asking you to help this event happen."

"I can't see him again." Tielle refused to give in to the shiver creeping up her back.

"Lord, child, was it *that* awful?"

"No, Des…that's the problem." Tielle pulled her arm free of Des's. "I should've turned him down flat when he asked me to do this but *as usual,* Grae snaps his fingers and I fall in line whenever he wants me. The man doesn't know what it sounds like to hear me say no."

"So teach him then, child." Desree bumped the younger woman's shoulder with her own.

Tielle's smile lost its glee to recapture despair. "The last time I tried that, he divorced me."

Tielle waited until after midnight to make good on her plans for escape. The word *coward* resounded in her head like a chime, but she didn't begrudge it. One day she was running her business, trying and failing to forget Graedon Clegg had ever been part of her life. The next day he was there talking to her as though the past year had never happened. Not to mention the fact that she was once again, and all too soon, surrounded by almost the entire Clegg clan. What was she supposed to do with all that? What could anyone do with all that?

Silently, she raged while making her way out by one of the many secluded staircases that wound through the big house. While she assumed most of her guests were asleep, or well on their way, she decided there was no sense using the most highly traveled areas to make a run for it.

None of this was necessary, Tielle knew that. She'd handled much tougher crews than the Clegg family while manning her business, yet the memories those people instilled only dredged up deeper ones of herself and Grae—memories she'd forced herself to shut away when what they'd had fell apart.

Tielle gave a quiet, triumphant sigh when she worked her way through the large, industrial-equipped kitchen. The staff garage was attached just off the area. She efficiently secured the door leading into the garage and headed through it to where she'd left her car parked outside earlier that day. Tossing her purse on the passenger seat of the Audi, she prepared to plant herself behind the wheel.

"Jeez, all this cloak-and-dagger stuff just to get out of spending a few days with my family, Tel?"

The wind had picked up, masking her gasp when Grae's rich octave cut through the air. She helped herself to a few deep breaths before closing the car door and turning to face the man, who was slyly grinning down at her from beneath a toboggan as dark as the whiskers shading his face.

"Don't try telling me you were doing anything other than making a run for it."

"Can you blame me?" Tielle shrugged, swatting at a lock of hair that slapped her cheek.

"It's that hard for you to be around them. Around me," he asked in that question-non-questioning way of his.

"What are you up to, Grae? Why would I want to be around any Clegg at all? *Especially* you?" She didn't raise her voice, yet the temper that had become increasingly difficult to manage over the past year came through as though amplified. "We're divorced, in case you forgot," she tacked on.

Aside from the erratic dance of a jaw muscle, he was utterly still. "Yeah, Ti, I forget that all the time."

"Well, it may be something you'll want to remember the next time you end a marriage." Her temper was on a slow simmer then.

Grae's own temper skipped simmer and dashed straight to boil, something it had done excessively during the past twelve months.

"Dammit, Tel." He invaded her space with an impressive swiftness for someone his size. "You weren't supposed to leave me." His voice was a gravel rumble that effectively unsettled most.

"*I* left *you?*" Her laughter was short, ill-humored. "That's good, Grae. Do you happen to recall that ultimatum of yours? 'Stop trying to fix things in my family, Tel. I'm the only one you should concern yourself with satisfying. Forget that one more time and consider us finished.'" The wind whistled as she recited the speech verbatim and then raised her hands defensively. "What was I supposed to do with that, Grae?"

Her words—*his* words—eased the rigid set to his shoulders. "You weren't supposed to let me get away with that ultimatum, dammit." His voice held its steely resilience. "You were supposed to tell me to go screw myself. You were supposed to lock me out of the bedroom, give me the silent treatment and then—"

"Do what you wanted me to anyway?" The anger left her voice to be replaced by a weak bewilderment.

"Don't leave, Tel." He crowded in a bit more.

The pressure of tears emerged. "We aren't going to fix things, Grae. Not here of all places, you know that."

"And *you* know I can't do *this* without you."

Curiosity added more sparkle to her eyes. "What do you mean?"

"I need you, Tel. I'm not—" He wasn't quite ready to admit that he wasn't strong enough. "I'm sorry for making you a part of the very thing I once ordered you to stay out of. As much as I don't want to do this with you, I can't do it without you."

Tielle considered him a moment and then shook her head. "I'm sorry, Grae. I'm not doing anything except getting the hell out of here unless you tell me what it is you can't do without me." Determinedly, she folded her arms across the teal sweatshirt she wore. "I want to know all of it, and I'll know if you're holding anything back."

Amen to that, Grae acknowledged and then went to lean against the side of Tielle's car.

"I don't have many details—"

"Grae…"

"I swear it." He spread his hands. "But Faro is up to something and—"

"This again…" Tielle muttered along with a curse. She reached for the driver's-side door handle, but Grae slid over before the door, effectively blocking the handle and absorbing her slight frame when she bumped into him.

Grae had unintentionally crushed Tielle against him, and she couldn't resist taking an unnecessarily deep breath. She thought of her nipples grazing his pecs and drew virtual pleasure from the memory. Tielle both celebrated and mourned the position. While it supported her—a thing her legs were incapable of just then—it sparked a potent tingle throughout her body, targeting her every nerve ending.

He proceeded to tell her what he knew, but Tielle could hear only the blood rushing through her ears. Her pounding heart provided accompaniment.

She sent a message to her brain. In it, she begged her eyes not to shut, thus clueing him in to how much his nearness affected her.

Cautiously, she curved her fingertips into the fabric of his shirt. The layers of clothing did relatively little to mask the unyielding plane of muscle that was his chest.

"I'm sorry, what?" she blurted when he called her name to recapture her attention. As she'd demanded, he'd given an explanation and was awaiting her response.

"When I figure all this out, I know I won't be able to confront my brother without you there with me."

Tielle hated herself for laughing, but her ex-husband's thought process prompted the action. "Have you thought about how well *that'd* go over? Your family doesn't need another reason to hate me, Grae."

"They don't hate you." His hands flexed on her arms at the notion.

"The women in your family would rather kick me than kiss me."

"None of the men feel that way." He sounded hopeful.

When she laughed and bowed her head, Grae dropped his easy expression to replace it with a tortured, needy one. Deeply, he inhaled the soft, floral scent of her hair. He could smell it through the fuzzy cap she wore. Taking further advantage of her closeness, he applied a subtle massage to her hips, cupping them faintly and then closing his eyes as though ordering himself not to do more.

"Can't you be wrong?" Her eyes were fixed on a fine strand loosed at the tip of his shirt's collar.

"I hope to heaven that I *am* wrong." He shrugged when her eyes flew to his face. "I want to feel what you do about Faro. I always have."

"Maybe if you told Faro—" She cut herself off when he shook his head.

"You know I won't."

"Why?"

"Because I can only even consider that when you're around me. Later, I won't even remember I said it."

Tielle shook her head. "Being around me didn't help much before, did it?"

He gathered her closer; the temperature had dipped several notches during their time outdoors. "When a man loses a lot, he starts to see things differently."

Grae trailed his fingers down her neck, *across* her collarbone. The tingles already affecting Tielle began to heat. Her lips parted, and she felt ready to offer him her tongue when the first sprinkle of snow landed on the tip of her nose.

"Damn you, Shanti Dillon."

Grae frowned playfully. "Who's that?"

"The weather lady."

"This may not be the best weather to drive in." He laughed.

Tielle gave the falling sprinkles a tired look. "I can still make it."

"Not if I take you inside first."

Her eyes narrowed as she read his thoughts. "Don't you dare. We'll wake the whole house."

"Not if you don't laugh the way you always do. It's a blow to my ego when you do that, you know?"

"Then don't—Grae!" Tielle shrieked when he bent and pulled her over his shoulder.

"My bag!" she screamed when he made a start for the garage door.

Grae carried her back to the car, setting her down so she could reach inside the car to grab the bag. He hooked a finger through a belt loop on her jeans to keep his possession secure. When Tielle grabbed her bag and tried to make a run for it, Grae slung her across his shoulder and carried his laughing ex-wife inside the house.

Chapter 4

Since rousing the rest of the Clegg family from their collective unconsciousness was the very *last* thing Tielle wanted to do, she stifled her desire to laugh, chuckle or even giggle as Grae returned her to her room. He carried her to the bed and followed her down, as she'd kept the collar of his navy flannel shirt in her grasp.

"How'd you know where I was sleeping?" Tielle asked, her cognac stare probing his bronze one.

"I make it my business to know these things."

"But you said I wasn't your business anymore."

Grae brought his full weight down upon her. "When will you stop taking everything I say so literally?"

Tielle relished the brunt of his body against hers. That time, she didn't command her eyes not to close. She savored the sensations he stirred and moved against him in a slow, needy grind.

Grae bowed his head. "Don't do that," he commanded in a whisper.

"Do what?" Tielle bit down on her lip and moaned close to his ear.

He grunted what sounded like a curse. Loosely cupping her neck, he used his thumb to tilt back her chin. Tielle followed through on giving him her tongue, and she didn't know which one of them whimpered first when their tongues tangled, engaging in a sultry duel.

Tielle had lost her cap during the unorthodox trip through the house, and her coarse locks were freed. Grae gathered a fistful of the dark mass, using his hold to keep her mouth crushed beneath his. She kept her hands filled with the material of his shirt, eager to take him out of it and paying little heed to what she was doing. She only wanted this—him—what she'd missed for well over a year.

Worry about the rest later, Ti, a voice silently reasoned.

Later sounded just as incredible to Grae. His palms were greedy to be full of her, and he set out with intentions of making that happen. He cupped and squeezed her breasts, which, while neatly encased beneath the hooded sweatshirt, were just as beckoning. They appeared to offer themselves to Grae with every breath Tielle took. The brief grinding moves she plied against him had him thrusting next to her and wishing their clothes were anywhere but covering them.

Grae grumbled something incomprehensible while scooping her bottom into his palms and lifting her more snuggly into his mock thrusts. Tielle shuddered. Her participation in the kiss had grown ragged, needier.

"Grae…" Her nails scraped the whiskers shading his jaw while their tongues danced.

He was helpless to stop, but eventually he managed to do just that. Ending the kiss, he pressed his face into the crook of her neck. "Keep forgetting you're not mine for the taking anymore."

"Why'd you come here, Grae?" she moaned. "You

could've sent anyone here to spy on Faro." Her eyes took on an accusing sheen. "Why'd you need to come here and upset things?"

"Upset things?" He laughed. "Don't you think things are already *upset* between us?"

Her lips thinned. "I'm dealing with it."

Grae smirked. "I'm not." He dropped a kiss to the corner of her mouth and left the room.

The next morning, Tielle studied her favorite bottle of creamer while preparing her first cup of coffee for the day. She wondered if she could get away with adding something a bit more flavorful to the hot beverage. She decided against that very appealing idea. Having gotten no sleep the night before, the last thing she needed was anything to induce relaxation.

"Hey! There you are! I've been looking for you since I got here," Laura called when she whirled into the smaller user-friendly staff kitchen. "I wanted to get your final approval for tonight's opening dinner."

Opening dinner. Tielle repeated the phrase in her head, not quite able—or willing—to believe they were still in the beginning stages of the family bonding event.

"Ti?" Laura looked concerned. She set her work portfolio aside and joined Tielle on the other side of the kitchen. "So how'd it go last night? I take it you decided against leaving."

With a withering look, Tielle took her coffee and went for a seat at one of the tables surrounding the kitchen island. Laura followed.

"I tried to leave…"

"Changed your mind?"

"May've had it changed for me." Tielle raised her mug

for a sip, decided against it. "Grae got here last night. Late."

Laura's gasp prefaced Grae's arrival in the kitchen. The man seemed riveted on his ex-wife but quickly recalled his immense charm and slanted a grin toward Laura.

"Lookin' good, miss," he called, meeting Laura at the opposite end of the island for a hug.

"Good to see you again. Tielle just told me you got here late last night." Laura's light caramel-toned face flushed a rich burgundy when she smiled up at Grae.

"Yeah, it was pretty late," he said. "Luckily, I got here in time to catch Tel before she ran off for the night."

Laura nodded. "Hope you're finding everything satisfactory?"

"Very satisfactory."

"And you'll let us know if there's anything you need."

"Count on it," he said, eyes fixed on Tielle.

Tielle cleared her throat suddenly. "Um, guys, I need to grab something from my office. The cooks left some bagels. Help yourself."

Rushing out, Tielle left Laura no reason to delicately make her exit. Smiling weakly, Laura looked to Grae, who waved a hand.

"Unnecessary," he said.

"Okay, I'm about to repeat myself," Laura said. "What happened last night?"

"I managed to make it through a full day with those people." Tielle fidgeted with the stylishly frayed hem of her emerald-green sweater. Sipping her coffee, she looked lovingly toward the wall bar in the office. "I waited till they were in dreamland before I tried to make it out of here. I was almost there when Grae stopped me—tried to talk me out of it."

"In the snow, how romantic…" Laura crooned.

"We didn't stay outside." Tielle's smile was indulgent. "Grae took me back to my room."

"Ah…where he tried to talk you out of it some more? Excuse me, not *tried*—succeeded. You *are* still here, after all."

Tielle ruffled her hair out of agitation and began to walk the office. "I was *this* close." She poised her thumb and forefinger centimeters apart. "I almost begged him. I—" She shook her head. "I was so lost in him and what he was…doing…"

"Oh, honey, don't be so hard on yourself. This is Grae, the man you love." She rolled her eyes dreamily. "A man any woman would love to have… Sorry—not much help, huh?"

"It's all right. But, Laura, I can't get caught up in him again." She stopped pacing and flopped on the side of the desk corner. "I wouldn't survive it. I'm hardly surviving it now. It—it's too much."

"Listen to me, Ti." Laura came over to join Tielle on the desk. "You're all over the place right now. This entire retreat hit you out of nowhere. You're entitled to be a little scattered."

"I've already told myself that." Tielle hugged herself. "I know it's true, but it is what it is. Grae being here is gonna make this week more insane than it already is."

"Then get out of here. Go." Laura nudged Tielle's shoulder with her own. "No one can blame you or make you stay."

"Grae's already asked me to stay. He says something's going on or about to happen and he needed me…" She slapped her knee. "Why'd I agree to it? Why can't I ever say no to him? And please—" she raised a hand to Laura "—don't say it's because I love him."

Laura gave a small smile. "Okay…"

Tielle dragged herself behind her desk and put her head down.

"As a man who can't stand any of his ex-wives, I now know what it feels like to see an ex you still love."

"I think I finally understand the phrase 'pleasure and pain.'" Grae topped off his OJ while speaking to Leo Cartright over the phone in the retreat's library.

"Do you realize this is the first time you haven't snapped at me for claiming you still love her?" Leo asked after a measure of silence.

"I'll give you one better." Grae sighed, browsing the library's shelves without actually reading the books' titles. "I didn't snap because it wasn't true—I snapped because I couldn't do anything about it."

"Do you *want* to do anything about it?"

"I want my wife back."

"Well, you're in the perfect place for it. You guys were married there, spent your honeymoon there."

Grae smiled. The idea held more appeal than Leo would ever imagine. "I've got other reasons for being here. How am I supposed to prove to Tel that I've changed when once again I have to play the role of big and bad for my family and while she's here to see me do it?"

"Why would you want her to stick around for that?" Leo asked, confusion evident in his voice.

Grae sipped his juice, and strolled on past the shelves. "It's one thing to handle board members, clients and the press—and another thing entirely to handle my family for something like this and with no anchor." He slipped a hand into a trouser pocket, clenched a fist. "Handling this without…my temper's getting worse, Leo."

"There's a chance you won't have to take this there."

"We both know I will, Leo."

"How are you gonna tackle it?"

"By waiting. He'll tip his hand sooner or later."

"Amen to that." Leo chuckled. "Boy never was any good at cards."

"Thanks, Leo," Grae said once their laughter had softened.

Tielle maintained her own set of rooms in the house. While she refused to be a workaholic, circumstances often called for her presence on the estate. During those occasions, the private area tended to be a godsend. Aside from Laura and a few select members of her medical staff, access to the third-floor wing was prohibited.

Either Grae didn't realize that or he just didn't care, Tielle mused when his lone knock sounded on the open door to her bedroom suite. It sent her whirling around to face him as she was heading to the bed from the closet to select an outfit for that night's family dinner.

"Not that one," he said, motioning to the frock she held. "My uncles won't be able to focus on a damn thing watching you bounce around in that all night."

Tielle schooled her expression, refusing to laugh, no matter how much she wanted to. "I don't bounce," she said instead.

The cool bronze of his gaze diluted to some warmer shade when it drifted down to survey the curvy frame encased in a snug, coral tank dress. "Okay," he muttered obediently.

"Did you overlook the sign that says Third-Floor Access Prohibited?"

"Not at all." Slowly, his gaze raked its way back up to her face. "Did you overlook the fact that I was here last night? You didn't seem to mind…granting me access then."

Tielle tossed aside the dress she carried, then retraced her steps to the walk-in closet. "What do you want, Grae? Get to it and get out." She'd just crossed into the closet when she felt him behind her. "Grae—"

"Get to it and get out, remember?" He slammed the closet door behind him.

"I won't do this."

"Do what?" He took her waist, lifted her close.

"I won't have sex with you while almost your entire family is in this house." She gritted her words through clenched teeth.

"Sex?" He let her slide down the length of him but kept her secure between a wall and his wide body. "Who said anything about sex? I only wanted to apologize for last night. My lack of respect, putting my hands on you in your own home without waiting for permission…"

"I don't have time for games, Grae."

"Neither do I, Tel." His expression left no room for playfulness. "But I need for you to understand this won't be easy for me. Sleeping down there—knowing you're up here…knowing how you smell."

He traced her cheek with the tip of his nose.

"Knowing how you feel…" His nose slid along the curve of her cheek, his thumb tracing a plump portion of bosom, rising up past the tank's square bodice.

"Knowing how you taste…"

Tielle could've melted back into the wall when his

lips, teeth and tongue performed a triple assault on her earlobe. "Why'd you let me walk away if…" The rest moaned into silence.

"This," he whispered amid his devastating feasting on her lobe, "was never our problem. But you're right, I *let* you walk away—that's all on me." His thumb outlined a slow circle around her nipple.

"Grae—"

"Let me take the blame for this, Tel. Let me remind myself what I have to do to fix this…" He slid his hand inside her bodice then, scooping out the breast and continuing the molestation of its nipple.

"Just understand that you're going to have to *tell* me not to touch you—not to taste you. Otherwise you'll damn well find yourself having sex with me while almost my entire family is in some part of this house."

He ceased the suckling at her lobe and fondling the breast he let remain outside the confines of her dress. Opening the door, he retreated a few steps and left her alone in the closet.

Tielle waited until she heard the room door close behind him. She made it as far as the chair in the center of the closet. Collapsing there, she waited for her emotions and everything else to settle.

Tielle finally accepted the fact that nothing she would choose for that evening's welcome dinner would keep her ex-husband's uncles on their best behavior. In truth, her concern wasn't for the gregarious group. Her concern was actually for her ex-husband. Grae had all but told her she'd be wise not to let herself be caught alone with him. That piece of advice, however, didn't pertain to the show of support Grae had requested she give in the presence of his family.

At that moment, Tielle was caught up in a...philosophical conversation with an older set of gentlemen. The discussion revolved around the logic of May-December romances.

"Younger cats are just too stupid to appreciate good things like you when they're bouncin' around right before their eyes."

Tielle laughed at Russell Clegg's point of view. "Mr. Russ, why is it that I don't get mad at you the way I did at Grae when *he* said I *bounce* around?"

"Well, Ti—" Russell shrugged, scratching at the top of his curly salt-and-pepper Afro "—you see, us older guys also have more style in our delivery."

The small crowd burst into hearty laughter that quieted when Grae joined the group. His hands went immediately to Tielle's hips. Smoothly, he cupped them, drawing her back until she was secure against him. Tielle caught the approving looks passing between the "older guys," but masked the sigh that begged for release.

"Grae?" She gave a pat to one of the cupping hands. "Could I talk to you for a second?"

The group had gathered in the living room, so Tielle led him into a parlor just off from the main den. Inside the small room, elegantly styled with an Oriental flavor that was depicted in the furnishings, throw rugs and art, she put a bit of distance between them.

"Grae, you can't do that," she said when he shut the door.

"Elaborate." He followed the movement of her hands across her hips accentuated by the pearl-gray material of the quarter-sleeved dress she'd chosen for the evening.

"I agreed to stand by you when the time comes for you to handle whatever you need to with your family, but all the rest—acting like we're still a couple—it's confusing...for everyone." *Especially me,* she tacked on silently, blinking rapidly to quell the sudden pressure behind her eyes. Privately, it was all confusing enough. In public, it was way too much.

Grae acknowledged her point with a slow nod and took a seat on the arm of a sofa. When he sighed and commenced massaging his neck, concern clouded Tielle's stare. She approached him at the sofa.

This was more than sibling upset, she realized. There was more wrong here than usual.

"You want to talk about it?"

Grae took her hand when she was within reach. "Remember the other day when I told you I wished I had your ability to see the best in people? I meant that, but I think my abilities run more along the lines of sniffing out the crap that people tend to pull." He toyed with her fingers. "I told you Faro wants you here because he wants to fix things wrong in the family and considers you part of the group." His hand flexed on hers. "May I tell you why *I* think he wants you here?"

He didn't look up to see her nod. "He knows putting you within one hundred feet of me is enough to keep me off-kilter. Given our current situation, it's enough to keep me oblivious to pretty much everything that's going on around me."

Tielle decided to pull back her hand, but Grae strengthened his grip a second before she moved.

"I've suspected for a long time that he's up to something," he said. "I've made moves to confront what he's got up his sleeve, and I pray I won't have to use them. My family's had to deal with enough drama, courtesy of me and Faro. Besides, there's a lot more I'd rather focus on."

Tielle watched him studying her fingers. She observed the wicked flex of muscle along his jaw when he traced her ring finger, which was bereft of his adornment.

"Grae…Faro only ever wanted you to be a brother," she softly encouraged.

"I was." Grae's smile was sad. "Just not the brother he wanted."

"Grae—"

"My family's terrified of me, Ti."

"Honey…" She moved closer, her heart breaking on what she heard in his voice. "No…"

"That horse's ass that masqueraded as your husband for the last eight months of our marriage, he's gotten worse. Some of them blame you for it." He pumped her hand. "That only makes me angrier."

The slow, rumbling breath he expelled stirred the fine hair along Tielle's nape.

"They love what my ability to coax and strong-arm has done for them financially. They just wish I'd tuck away the crazy alpha during family get-togethers."

"I fell in love with that crazy alpha," Tielle confessed.

"I know you did." He nodded. "You tamed me. But I think I've got more rough edges now than you could ever tolerate. That's gonna make it harder for me to get my ring back on your finger." His hand tightened on hers when she attempted to withdraw her own.

"You know I want you back," he said. "I never wanted you to go and you know I have no qualms about doing what I have to to get you back where you belong."

"Grae, you've got your family to deal with and all

this you're saying about us—you're trying to deal with us being around each other—"

"Stop, Tel. Don't do that. You know that's not it." He pinned her with a long stare. "You don't have to admit it, but don't play the role like you're good with the way we are."

"All right. But this isn't the time to discuss it."

"Fair enough, but you know it's coming."

Tielle could only confirm that with a shaky breath.

Grae lifted her hand, holding it to his mouth for a time and then grazing a kiss across her knuckles. Then her wrist...

She flexed her fingers next to his cheek and leaned in helplessly when his tongue bathed the pulse point at her wrist. The damp kiss traveled to her palm, the tips of her fingers...

Grae sitting on the arm of the sofa put them eye to eye. He only needed to tug once in order to bring her mouth full against his.

The kiss began with a series of quick, sweet pecks. Gradually, their lips parted, tongues just barely peeking past and then seeking, finding, nudging and entwining.

"Grae..."

"Make me stop."

She pretended not to hear the tortured warning. She deepened her exploration of his talented mouth and moaned in a manner that was undeniably ego stroking.

Chapter 5

"You're gonna have to stop me, Ti…"

"I will…"

Tielle made no moves to stop him. She didn't seem to be interested in stopping anything, especially when Grae tugged her closer so that she was straddling his lap during their kiss. His hands skimmed her waist and curved down to cup and squeeze her ample bottom when sudden knocking fell to the parlor door.

Murmuring something indecipherable, Tielle was kneading Grae's broad shoulders beneath the midnight-blue jacket he wore over a shirt of the same color. Stopping wasn't on her mind, only her consideration for pushing Grae to his back on the sofa.

"Dinner!" someone announced through the door.

Cheeks burning, Tielle took note of her situation and disentangled herself from Grae. The iron bands of his arms tightened before she could completely disengage.

"Fix this," he said, brushing his thumb across her lipstick-smudged mouth. He provided her with a tissue from a decorative dispenser perched on the table behind the sofa.

Tielle accepted without looking toward him and disappeared into the parlor's private room.

* * *

"Hands off," she murmured when he escorted her to her place at the long dining table.

"Yes, ma'am," Grae obliged with a meekness no one would believe.

Desree Clegg was seated across from the couple. The approval in her expression was impossible to miss.

"It's not what you think," Tielle explained.

"Humph," Desree laughed. "You don't believe that any more than I do."

The sound of a fork clinking crystal echoed in the room, and the soothing rumble of mixed conversation quieted. Heads turned toward the end of the long table where Faro Clegg stood smiling out over his family.

"Thank you, all, for arranging your schedules to be free," Faro said.

"Good timing, man," Oscar Clegg called out. "Chances are we'll be snowed in by the end of the week."

Grae heard Tielle groan softly over his uncle's prediction. With a cool smile, he patted her thigh beneath the table and let it remain there to apply a slow massage. Tielle reciprocated by patting his hand and removing it.

"I hope our time in this place will be done before any real snow falls," Faro said from the head of the table, "but I can't think of a lovelier place to be stranded. I'd like to take this time to thank Tielle and her staff for opening the place on such short notice."

With that acknowledgment, Faro applauded. The gesture was followed by less than half of the assembled group.

"Guess you're all wondering why we're here?" Faro queried once the pitiful claps silenced into murmurs of agreement. "This family runs one of the most successful marketing firms in the nation, but I'm sure none of us are blind to the fact that those successes almost equal many of our failures as a family."

The murmurs gained volume. Their agreeing tones, however, betrayed signs of agitation.

"I know that I have much to answer for, and if I can admit that, can't all of you?"

The low murmuring of voices silenced as though a switch had been hit. The group looked to Faro with greater interest, heightened suspicion.

"Stay with me, guys," Faro urged. "There's drama in this family that's been around since I was a kid, and I can remember a time when it wasn't like that. I was old enough to remember the love we all used to have for each other."

"Talk plain, Faro. What'd you really bring us up here for?" Paul Clegg demanded.

"Because I'm ready to be honest and lay it on the line about my shortcomings. I want you all to do the same."

"What's that gonna solve?" Ken Clegg's youngest brother, Barry, asked.

"Yeah, Faro, and why did we all have to come out to Tielle's stuck-up psychiatric ward to talk about it?" Asia complained.

"Because there's been enough talking behind closed doors," Faro countered.

"What do you expect us to admit?" Grae asked.

The room stilled. The group was nervously expectant, as was usually the case whenever the brothers conversed.

"We need to discuss where things went wrong." Faro's voice sounded fuller. "Where they went wrong and why, and give apology where apology is due."

"What the hell are you talkin' about, boy?" Russell

Clegg's question launched heated discussions that colored the dining room with tense language and harsh laughter.

"Could you give us some example of what you mean for us to do, Faro?" Desree's easy tone somehow cut through the melee.

Some silenced their agitated words while others leaned forward in anticipation of Faro's reply. Instinctively, Tielle sought Grae's hand, clutching it beneath the table.

"I want to apologize for coming between one of the happiest couples I know," Faro said.

As Tielle had predicted, all eyes turned toward herself and Grae.

With his family looking on, Grae watched his brother do something he'd never witnessed—take responsibility for his own wrongdoing.

Faro's expression was earnest. "Tielle, I'm sorry for making you feel so torn, at odds with yourself for doing what you thought was right and what was best for your marriage. I should've told you it wasn't your place, refused your help." He looked to his brother. "Grae, I should've gone along with your wishes to keep her out of it. If I'd helped you put up a united front, things may've been a lot simpler and it all never would've gone as far as…badly as it did."

Faro hid his hands in his walnut-colored trouser pockets. "I've apologized before, but never really came clean with any real depth and before the eyes and ears of our family. Tielle, Grae, I'm sorry."

Faro allowed a span of time to pass between them before he once again addressed the group. "It's as simple as that, folks. Admit to the wrongdoings and the parts we played in damaging our family."

"You're making it hard to be blackmailed, that's for damn sure."

There was some laughter at Barry's words, but not much. Faro smiled wanly.

"Family, sooner or later all the ugliness will catch up to us. Then it'll ooze over with the business and bring tension there, as well," he said. "I'm surprised it hasn't happened already. Surprised Grae can still work with me, much less look at me. I've had enough, but that doesn't matter if none of the rest of you have."

"Where's all this coming from, Faro?" Jill Clegg asked. "We aren't all at each other's throats. If anything, you and Grae do more squabbling than anyone."

"Amen," Asia supported her great-aunt's claim, "and I wonder why that is."

"Asia…" Ranata warned her cousin.

"You wonder why?" Faro challenged his cousin's words, a glare bringing his dark face into further shadow. "Anybody could feel the coldness in the family after a certain point."

"Faro?" Desree's expression was both curious and haunted. "Honey, what in the world are you talking about?"

"And how do you know about any coldness in the family?" Jill challenged. "You're a child."

"I'm old enough to remember it," Faro argued.

"You ain't that old," Russell snapped.

"Is this what you dragged us out here for, boy?" Paul frowned. "To rehash some drama you think you sensed when you were a kid?"

"Can any one of you say this family has no issues?"

Faro asked, his patience with his family showing signs of strain.

"All families have issues, honey." Desree's reminder was soft.

"Damn right," Asia blurted. "And none that require a bloated getaway in some overpriced resort."

"And that's enough for me." Tielle sighed, her voice holding a trace of happy relief. She stood.

"Please, sweetie," Desree urged with a poised wave, "don't go. We haven't even had the chance to enjoy our delicious meal yet."

"I know, Des." Tielle managed a soft smile in the woman's direction. "But I've had more than enough."

Asia gasped at the comment as Tielle threw down her napkin and left the dining room. Grae decided not to follow his ex-wife even though he wanted to. He'd go to her shortly, but he wanted to stay and observe his brother.

There was something more in motion then, he realized. Whatever he and Leo had suspected may have had merit, but it was in no way the endgame.

So much for swooping in to save the day, he thought.

It seemed he'd have no other choice than to wait for Faro to reveal his hand. That meant spending less time tending to what he'd really come there for—Tielle.

Dinner turned out to be more of a touch-and-go event than it was intended to be. No one complained. Faro's attempt to have the family share its deepest and darkest had most certainly backfired. Still, the man tried his best to salvage what he'd planned for the night. He'd apparently hoped that a change of venue might loosen tongues, but instead the family made silent choices to help themselves at the impressive buffet and then to enjoy meals in the privacy of their respective suites.

Given that course of action, Tielle opted for remaining downstairs. Following her stormy departure from the dining room, she took refuge in the library, which had always been one of her favorite places to retreat to. She had one of the cook staff deliver her dinner there. The chill of the evening made it suitable to build a fire, so Tielle curled up on the sofa in front of the enormous hearth. The structure spanned a broad portion of the wall beneath the library's second level of bookcases.

She was indulging in the first course—a hearty, gooey potato soup—when the wide cherrywood door creaked open to admit Grae's tall frame. In one hand, he balanced a wooden tray that carried large portions of that evening's meal. In his other hand, he carried a large mug of frothy beer, which he gulped from while making his way into the library.

Tielle smiled, realizing he believed he was alone in the big space. "Hello," she said once he'd set down the tray.

Grae turned with surprising swiftness for a man his size. "Tel," he breathed out.

"Did I scare you?" she asked.

"Relieved me."

She laughed. "Sorry."

"No need. *I'm* the one who should be apologizing."

Tielle only waved a hand. "There's been enough apologizing for one night." She focused on stirring her soup.

"Definitely," Grae agreed and then motioned to the sofa she occupied. "You mind?"

Tielle continued to stir. "Will I find myself on my back if I let you sit next to me?"

His low, easy chuckles filled the room. "That won't

happen for at least another half hour. I'm too hungry and aggravated to put you in any compromising positions."

"Ah…so that's the secret…" Tielle savored a spoonful of soup.

"Secret's right, so keep it to yourself," Grae playfully suggested.

"Whatever works, right? I think I feel better being tucked away in my favorite place."

"That's why I'm here," Grae said. "I remember how much you always enjoyed it, thought some of that might rub off."

"Grae, how long do you think everyone's gonna tolerate Faro's bonding time before they hit the road?"

"Hard to say." Graedon cut into one of the thick bourbon scallion chicken strips. "I think everybody's still too curious about what he's up to." He winced. "Sorry for sounding suspicious."

"I think you're right." Tielle stirred the creamy soup. "The situation calls for a fair amount of suspicion."

Her admission caught Grae off guard. "Do tell," he urged.

She shrugged and enjoyed another helping of soup. "Something feels off."

"Insincere?"

"I don't know…forced somehow, maybe? Like he's looking for something."

"Yeah…" Grae spoke around the cream spinach pinwheel he'd just popped into his mouth.

"Guess it's still too early to get any real line on what he's after. We'll probably be here the whole time trying to get to the bottom of it."

"Great." Grae's agitation was more pronounced over

the realization of how far he was from tackling the issues between himself and Tielle.

They ate in silence for a time. When they'd had their fill of dinner, they remained on the sofa. The fire's raging intensity worked its magic, weighing their eyelids, rendering their bodies boneless as relaxation set in.

Overnight, the promised heavy snow set in. The atmosphere provided perfect sleeping weather, but in Desree Clegg's room, sleep wasn't in session. Des sat around a coffee table laden with all the fixings for a well-stocked tea party. Joining her were three of her cousins.

Conversation had taken a backseat to delighting in the array of teas and fattening pastries decorating the table. Slowly, discussion worked its way back into the gathering.

"I think we should thank him for treating us to a dazzling weekend and then hit the road first thing in the morning," Desree said.

Layla snorted. "This is a gorgeous place, Des, and Faro's footin' the bill. No need to act too hasty." She added another cream Danish to her saucer. "And that snow's been coming down steady for over an hour. Chances are good the road's been cut off, anyway."

"That's a good point," Shelly Clegg agreed. "Faro's just tryin' to find a way to improve Grae's awful mood by apologizing in front of all of us and masking it behind group healing." She twisted a still-pouty mouth. "Get us to reveal our mess and make his look better than it is."

Desree sipped from her cup and held it as if hoping to draw calm from the warmth penetrating the ceramic. "I have a feeling it's more than that." Her tone was reflective, haunted.

"There she goes, y'all," Janie Clegg groaned. "Des and her conspiracy theories."

Laughter roared at Desree's expense for a time.

"He's always been a crafty child," Des pointed out through her own laughter. "Doesn't do anything without a reason behind it, and I'm not willing to say that tonight was just about him apologizing to Tielle and Grae. He could've had a family dinner at his house for that."

Desree's point of view appeared to take hold. Silently, the group contemplated the logic of it all.

"What reason would he have?" Layla asked.

Desree flexed her fingers around her mug and sighed. "Guess we'll have to wait until he shows more of the hand he's holding."

While the oversized sofa before the library fireplace could fit two people quite nicely, its ability to do so was terribly strained when one of those people was Grae. He and Tielle had taken up opposite ends of the long chair. Grae's legs stretched along the length of Tielle's smaller frame, providing wonderful support for her back while she dozed on her side.

Grae had been first to awaken from the nap they'd fallen into after dinner. The fire wasn't roaring quite so furiously, yet it presented its enthusiastic flames and a seeking warmth from the wide hearth. The vibrancy of those flames, however, was still unsuccessful at capturing Grae's attention when it competed against the sight of Tielle at rest.

Inching closer, he eased one leg off the sofa, careful to keep the other behind Tielle's slumbering form. He thought over how often he'd planned a trip to Vancouver over the past year…and what became of those plans. Now he was there, and she was within touching distance. He smoothed a few fingers through her hair. He was there with her, and they were caught up in family melodrama, of all things. The reality of it was turning him inside out.

Grae's fingers gently stroked through her unbound hair, which was held back from her face by a thin braid wrapped about her head. Tielle fidgeted, on the verge of waking. She turned on her back, the move forcing open the bodice of the casual quarter-sleeved frock she'd worn for dinner. The hem had already risen to a suggestive position along her thigh. The V-neck bodice parted to reveal glimpses of the perfect breasts he'd missed.

"Dammit, Tel." The curse was playful, albeit tortured. She dozed with no clue or care for how insane she was driving him.

"Ti." He prayed she'd awakened before his lack of restraint asserted itself. "Tel."

He rubbed her thigh, telling himself it was merely to help her waken, when every stroke only sent the hem of her dress higher.

She shifted again and sent his hand sloping to her inner thigh. Completely her fault, of course. Then, as if she hadn't tortured him enough, a faint sigh escaped her parted lips as though she were thoroughly and beautifully relaxed.

He leaned close to whisper, "Honey, wake up for me."

All the while, the hand at her inner thigh smoothed closer to what he hungered for. The pad of his thumb commenced a slow assault along the folds of her sex, still secure inside her panties. His thumb glided slowly up and down the cottony fabric. Grae felt his eyelids growing heavy as sensation stirred wildly inside him.

He left off the urgings for her to awaken, preferring

to dry-suckle her petal-soft earlobes as his touch to the middle of her panties grew more insistent. Tielle's movements on the sofa took on a new intensity. Grae let loose a groan, feeling the subtle arch of her hips when she offered herself to him.

Offered herself to him?

She's asleep, for God's sake, he berated himself, yet he made no effort to remove his offending fingers. Her smell tantalized him, reminded him. He'd missed her so. Why did he let it all go so far?

Squeezing his eyes shut tightly, he refused to let such regrets infiltrate the pleasure hazing his brain. He could just feel slight dampness seeping through the material of her most intimate apparel.

His mouth went dry for wanting her. He wanted his mouth there at her entrance to drink in the sweet milk of her need. He wanted to inhale her exquisite aroma and lose himself inside the tight well of her desire.

"Babe, wake up." He clenched a fist, resisting the need to take his touch to a deeper level.

Seconds later, the decision was taken from him. Tielle gripped his wrist in one hand and guided his fingers with the other.

Chapter 6

"Tel, I—"

Her sudden movement sent apology to his tongue until he understood her intentions.

"Tel?" His tone was uncertain, and he felt like an absolute heel for arousing her from her sleep.

It was, of course, a thing he'd done many times during their marriage. Those nights he'd return late from the firm, from a meeting about a new campaign, from arguing with his brother... He'd come home to find her asleep and toy with her until she woke and gave him what he craved.

He'd never felt like a heel for doing it before.

Guess there's a first time for everything, he thought.

The fact that Tielle was asleep, however, was still up for debate. She gripped him with a surprising strength for someone under the veil of sleep.

"Tel?" His head dipped closer, and he attempted to observe her captivating face.

The fire still blazed, though not with quite as much fervor as it had earlier. Her face remained shadowed, yet Grae could see that her eyes were closed—out of pleasure or drowsiness, he could not be sure.

A mixture of both, perhaps?

He received his answer moments later when the softest cries radiated up from her throat, past the sultry part of her pouted lips. Whether deep in sleep or on the verge of waking, she was apparently lucid enough to have insinuated his middle finger inside her panties. Inside…her.

Mouthing curses, Grae shut his eyes and let himself be taken by undeniable satisfaction as he touched her, *really* touched her. He grunted a little as his finger slid higher. She was dousing his skin with her need, and he wondered how in heaven he'd done without her for over a year.

She was murmuring something—the same word wrapped up in a moaning cry. It nudged Grae right to sanity's edge when he realized she was chanting his name. Her hips arched slowly, steadily, and her thighs parted wider to receive every inch of his finger.

Grae used his thumb to stimulate the nub of flesh just slightly above her center. Arrogant approval sent a smirk tugging at the curve of his mouth as her cries gained breadth and volume. He didn't care who overheard. This was a treat he'd been denied for far too long.

Tielle's eyes flew open suddenly. Their inviting cognac depths seemed to stir with equal parts astonishment and delight before her lashes settled as she crested on the waves of exquisite pleasure he kindled.

Her chanting cries resumed, gaining volume, and then Grae *did* mind who might overhear them. He wanted no interruptions, and as they hadn't thought to lock the library door…

"Babe…shh…" His nose nuzzled hers, his tongue outlining the plump curve of her mouth once, twice, and then delving inside to tangle with hers.

Tielle was a happy participant in the kiss, though she intermingled moaning Grae's name in the midst of it. Intimate, indulgent conversation flowed then—softly and intended only for their ears.

"Don't stop," she sobbed.

"Keep your voice down."

Her soft laughter surged.

"I didn't mean to wake you," he said.

"Liar," she countered.

Grae deepened the kiss while filling Tielle with another thick finger that sent her shrieking on the cusp of climax. Not to be outdone, Tielle extended a shaky hand, her intention to release the gleaming silver buckle securing the belt at the jeans he'd chosen to dress down the shirt and jacket he wore that evening. The jacket had been tossed over the back of the sofa some time ago.

Grae murmured her name during the kiss. He was torn between sampling what his fingers explored and somehow exercising caution. She deserved more than a quick round of satisfaction from a man who had walked away because she wouldn't bow to his will.

The lusty thrusting of his tongue on hers began to show signs of cooling. Infrequently, he sighed her name, but Tielle was in no frame of mind—or body—to hear words that hinted of anything other than those of the most pleasurable variety.

"Grae, please." She put his free hand to the breast almost bared past the bodice of her dress. She arched, biting down hard on her bottom lip when exquisite sensation lanced through her from the spot where her nipple grazed the middle of his palm.

"Hell…" Grae's voice was ragged and low, yet he managed to turn the tables and clutched Tielle's hand then. He secured Tielle's hand near her head.

Again, Tielle's eyes flew open. She frowned. "What's wrong?" She could feel his ardor cooling.

"Not this way. Not here," he said.

"Do you want to go to my room?"

He chuckled. "Not quite what I meant."

"Your room?" She sounded hopeful.

"Both rooms."

Her expression turned gleeful.

"Separately."

Glee transitioned to disappointment.

"I can walk you," he offered.

"I don't want you to walk me. I want you to—"

"Tel…"

She rolled her eyes, knowing what it sounded like when his mind was made up and would remain unchanged. She pushed at the hand that had been treating her so beautifully. It had turned into a cold reminder of what she was being denied.

Heated, Tielle fixed her clothes while scooting from the sofa. "Don't bother. I can walk myself."

"Tel, babe." He set a hand to her waist. "Don't go away mad."

"Don't worry, Grae. Mad isn't all I am." She shoved him aside and left the sofa, storming out of the library in her bare feet.

Graedon claimed the spot Tielle had just vacated. Resting his head on the sofa's arm, he groaned.

"So how'd you leave things with her?"

"I'm pretty sure she's somewhere in this house still cursing me."

Leo's chuckles deepened as they had since the onset

of his phone call with Grae. "It's never a good thing to have a woman *that* fine pissed at you."

"I got that part, Leo. If you could give me the trick for getting her *un*pissed, I'd be grateful."

Leo's sigh wasn't reassuring. "If I knew that answer, I'd not be thrice divorced."

The two had been talking for over a half hour that morning. Grae had been up since well before sunrise after a night of restless sleep. Sleep? He doubted he'd closed his eyes for more than twenty minutes once he'd finally returned to his room.

Thoughts of Tielle angry with him, however, weren't the only things jockeying for space in his cluttered mind. He'd also called to discuss his brother's weirder-than-normal behavior the night before.

"It was like he was hinting at something, but trying to veil it behind confusion," Grae said once the conversation had returned to Faro. "I got the impression he already knew whatever it was he wanted the rest of the group to own up to."

"So he just came at everybody with this and demanded they join him in this cleansing session?" Leo asked, following several quiet moments.

"He said something about things…changing in the family after a certain point."

"What?" Leo's voice hitched on something akin to astonishment in addition to curiosity.

Grae didn't notice, owning Leo's query up to proof of surprise over Faro's increasing aptitude for strangeness. Besides, he was too weary to wax on conspiracy theories. After all, he was in the midst of hungering insatiably for his wife—ex-wife—and trying to concoct a way to win her back while surrounded by his drama-prone family.

"Did anything else seem off?" Leo asked.

Grae's sigh rounded out into a groan. "Whatever this supposed *change* is about, apparently it all happened when we were kids."

"He said that? Grae? What'd he say exactly?"

"Come on, Leo, you know him. A bunch of nothin'." Grae scratched at his muscle-packed abdomen and silently summoned the will to push out of bed.

"What *exactly* did he say?"

Leo's insistence succeeded in drawing Grae from the tousled covers. "He said drama in our family has been around since he was a kid. He could recall a time when it wasn't like that. Said he was old enough to remember the love we used to have for each other. That verbatim enough for you?"

"Keep me posted, all right?" Leo urged.

Grae didn't seem to notice the hollow element in his uncle's voice. "There's some kind of group session with the retreat's therapists tonight," he went on, relaying the events on tap. "Won't *that* be loads of fun…"

Grae's obvious sense of foreboding seemed to ease a bit of Leo's dread. "Remember the best part is that you're getting to see more of Tielle than you have in a year."

"Yeah…" Grae settled onto one of the two armchairs in the bedroom alcove. There, he bowed his head and conjured the image of Tielle from the night before. The missed beauty of her breasts and arousing curves…the way she felt next to him, how she sounded in his ear as he pleasured her…it definitely wouldn't be difficult to recall the best parts about being there.

"Keep me posted, all right?" Leo repeated the instruction and ended the conversation seconds later.

Grae set his mobile on the windowsill before propping his bare feet on the accompanying armchair. He massaged his eyes and then directed his gaze toward the ceiling. He thought of what he'd said to Tielle about being in his assigned room while she was just there above him and within walking distance.

It would all have to wait, he knew, until Faro showed his colors and they could get to the bottom of what the weekend was supposed to be about. Obviously, the man was one for drawing out the suspense. That wouldn't help much in terms of getting to what he was most interested in.

Perhaps it'd be a little helpful to give his brother a slight nudge toward revealing his hand earlier. He'd done it before, Grae recalled. Of course, it was always easiest before an audience. A smile defined the curve of his smile as an idea took hold.

"Des!" Faro greeted his aunt warmly as they both entered the dining room for breakfast that morning. He gestured for her to precede him into the lovely room. The place was utterly inviting, heated comfortably by the healthy blaze churning in the hearth.

"Thank you," Desree said. "Wonderful location." She hooked the strap of a lavender tote over a chair at the table she'd selected. "I can't think of a lovelier place for an event like this."

Faro seemed taken aback. "I thought you'd be a little ticked at me for dragging Tielle into our family drama."

A little smile crossed her face as she prepared her coffee at the buffet. "You've got as much unfinished business with her as anyone, and she's very well aware of our *family drama*. We should be able to depend on her for discretion at the very least."

"That's true," Faro agreed, as if Desree's reason was one he had not considered. "Well, I hope the rest of the family will follow my lead and own up to whatever issues they need to get off their chests."

Desree tested her coffee and decided a touch more sugar was needed. "Are you so sure they will?"

Faro had approached the buffet to fill a plate with bacon and potatoes. "Nothing will ever get back to normal if they don't."

Des observed him. "What do you mean 'back to normal'? What exactly constitutes *normal* in your mind?"

Faro added a few more spoonfuls of the breakfast potatoes to his plate and followed up with chunks of cantaloupe and grapes. "There's a tension that's slowly weaved its way through the family. It's been destroying us little by little ever since."

Desree had finished doctoring her coffee and gaped at her nephew. "What *is* this tension, Faro? You say you've been aware of it since you were a child?"

Still preparing his plate, Faro smirked. "I thought that'd get the attention of certain folks."

"Why was that important?" Desree's expressive brown eyes narrowed.

Faro shrugged. "It wasn't."

"But it was something you were aiming for?"

"Des!" Faro laughed. "Why so serious? This weekend isn't about that, you know?"

"Is that right? Because it sounded pretty serious last night."

"Because you all are making it that way." Some of the lightness in Faro's voice had dissolved.

Desree nodded, folding her arms across the front of the knit plum sweater she wore. "*You're* the one who invited us all out here. Clearly there's a reason, and evidently it's a reason that's been a source of tension for the family. Tell me what part of that isn't serious, Faro?"

"Des, this time away is about confronting all the dirty little items that have managed to divide the family over the years." Faro's voice held a resolved tinge. "I, for one, believe that sharing those items could be the beginning of much-needed healing for the family." He shrugged.

"No, that might not be the same mode of thought that others have." He returned to filling his plate. "Maybe there are those of you who think there are some things best left untreated."

"Nerves grow numb after a time, Faro." Desree walked slowly with her coffee back to the table. "Aggravating them once that happens rarely does anything except to inflict pain. Or is that what you're aiming for, boy?" She kept her back to him while posing the charge.

The veiled accusation removed any phony enhancements of politeness Faro had worked to keep in place. "You're asking what I'm aiming for?" He set aside his plate, never taking his eyes from Des, whom he regarded with a mixed blend of precaution and slyness. "I'm aiming for quite a few things, Desree. Some to cause problems neither you nor I want." He smiled. "Still not quite sure what I mean, huh? Maybe after a few more family get-togethers you'll have a better idea, and that might make you think about how you can spare the family some of that drama."

The room started to fill with other family members. Faro finished with his plate and called out to the others in a voice of welcome. Desree wondered if anyone noticed how insincere it sounded.

"Eat up, everybody! We got lots on tap for the day," Faro said.

"Things gonna get weird like they did last night?" someone asked.

"Let's hope not." Faro eased a quick knowing look toward Desree.

"Is it me or are you hiding?" Laura asked when she entered Tielle's office and leaned on the door.

"Why would you think that?" Tielle rolled her eyes when Laura sent a pointed look toward her platter of coffee, breakfast potatoes, bacon and fruit. She shrugged. "Thought I'd get more done in here."

"Right."

Tielle shook her head, smiled. "Did you hear about last night's dinner?"

"Bits and pieces. Enough to know you were pretty pissed over it. Walked out before dessert—is that right?"

"Humph. Walked out before dinner."

Laura whistled. "That bad, huh?"

"That bad."

"How'd Grae take it?"

"We wound up having dinner together in the library." Tielle broke a bacon strip in half.

Laura's eyes widened. "What was that like?"

"We fell asleep on the sofa after dinner."

"And?" Laura settled onto the arm of a chair. "Did it end there?" Her hope that it hadn't was obvious.

"Didn't have to, but he…" Tielle studied her breakfast with sudden distaste. "He pulled back." Taking her mug, she left the sofa. "He wants to fix things, to make it up to me for driving us to divorce."

Laura traced one of the pleats in her brick-colored

skirt. "Does he plan to keep his distance until he's done that?"

"It's hard to sway him once he's made up his mind. Looks like he thinks it's best to stay away." Tielle stood before the beverage cart, cup in hand.

"And where do *you* stand in all this?"

Kicking herself into movement, Tielle sugared her coffee and laced it with a heavy dose of cream. "I stand on the side of right," she triumphantly announced and then gave a cold laugh. "At least that's how Grae sees it. He won't let me take responsibility for any of it."

"Is that a bad thing?" Laura blinked.

"When we were married, he *asked* me—" Tielle returned to the sofa and cluster of arm chairs designating the office living area "—*asked* me to stay out of trying to revamp his relationship with his brother. His *asking* meant I had the option of declining, which I did.

"I did everything I could to bring him and Faro closer even after he stopped *asking* me to stay out of it and *told* me to." She slapped a hand to the side of her pencil mocha-colored skirt. "Now we're divorced and he expects me not to take the blame for *any* part of that."

"Honey, we've talked about this before." Laura leaned forward. "You already know it would've been next to impossible for you to abide by that, no matter how he asked you to. This is who you are. It never would've turned out any other way than it did."

Tielle settled into one of the chairs flanking the sofa. "Grae being here every day isn't the only reason I can't let it go." She sipped from her coffee, relished the taste hitting her tongue and swallowed.

"Faro wants the family to come clean about everything that's driven them apart over the years. The night started passably enough, but then it swerved off course and went someplace no one seemed sure of except Faro."

Laura exchanged her place on the arm of the chair for the seat cushion itself. "What are you saying, Ti?"

"All those years ago, I didn't stick up for Faro because I was just a bighearted fool, or because helping's just in my blood, or because I was trying to live up to some standard my grandparents had put in place." She rubbed her hands against suddenly chilled arms bared by the capped sleeves of a black sweater. "I did it because he struck me as a man who'd been a horrible big brother, and he finally wanted to make it up and repair a relationship he'd destroyed."

Laura appeared bewildered. "Are you saying you think he's no longer interested in getting things right with him and Grae?"

"No, Laura." Tielle's smile was sad. "I'm saying that I don't think he was *ever* interested in getting things right with Grae."

Laura's bewilderment cleared as she straightened on the chair. "When did this occur to you?"

"Something about him last night." Tielle slumped back in the chair and let her hands dangle over the arms. "I never noticed it before in all the times I talked to him. Guess that's because I never spent much time around him in a family setting—certainly none like what we're so privileged to be part of now."

Tielle rested her head back on the chair. "Last night I felt like I was looking at a stranger, Laura, and if I was wrong about Faro, that means I jeopardized my marriage for nothing."

Chapter 7

Since breakfast that morning was set to be more of a drop-in affair, Tielle made no effort to...*drop in*. Not that she'd had any intention to do so regardless. Following her chat with Laura, she decided that to venture completely outside the house would be a better plan. She was willing to try anything that would save her from running into those members of the Clegg family who still had a cross word or an evil eye to throw her way.

Grae found his ex-wife bundled on one of the cushioned chairs outside the pool cottage. "Being around my family is so bad you'd rather brave these morning temps," he noted.

She smiled, but kept her eyes on the screen of her tablet. "Being around your family is so bad, I'd rather brave these morning temps," she confirmed.

"Still pissed." He phrased the question in his usual manner of statement.

Tielle didn't lift her head from the work she studied. "Still such a slave to your ego that you think me denying myself the full pleasure of your company means I'm pissed at you?"

"You've avoided me all day."

She almost laughed. "It's still the morning!"

"Tel…" he virtually purred while easing both hands into the front pockets of the white fleece hoody he sported. "You know how much I like to 'get up' early."

"That's right…" She ignored the suggestion in his words. "It's still sex on your terms, your time…"

"Well, you never took the initiative." Grae chuckled.

Tielle laughed then, as well. "There was never any need!"

He blinked, a stricken look befalling his finely crafted face. "Was that a problem for you?" he asked in a small voice.

"No, Grae, it never was." Her expression was soft when she looked at him. "We only had one major problem."

"True, but it was a major problem that shined a harsh light on all the rest."

"Do you really think we can magically work out our issues, topped off by divorce and a year apart?"

"I don't think magic is the answer."

Tielle shut down her tablet. "What is?" she asked.

"This place." Grae spared a moment to study the sun-kissed expanse of gardens beyond the sunken pool area. "I can't think of a better place to find what we lost than the place it all began."

Tielle couldn't deny the strength of his logic, nor the chill it sent through her despite the layers of her sweatshirt, tank top, jeans and the wool blanket atop them.

Memory took her back to a day eight years prior when Clegg Marketing, then led by Kenneth Clegg, had its first executive staff retreat. They selected Turner Estates and Gardens for the venue.

Tielle had arrived in time for a late supper with her grandmothers and was introduced to Ken's son, Grae.

Tina and Danielle had already taken an extreme liking to the young man, whom they invited to stay and enjoy supper with them and their granddaughter.

Grae knew he would've accepted the offer regardless. Tina and Danielle had an aura about them that would have appealed to any man. When Tielle arrived halfway through the first course, Grae had no desire to dine elsewhere for the duration of the retreat or until Tielle left the estate. He had been utterly fascinated by the curvy, dark beauty, and they'd spent the next three weekends together. By then, he had tumbled headfirst into love with her. Two years later they were married, four years after that they were divorced.

Grae shook his head on the memory, grateful for the interruption of Tielle's ringing phone. He listened in as she greeted and chatted with Laura Cooper. Laura's contribution to the discussion must not have been good, for Tielle rolled her eyes a few moments into the conversation.

"We've been summoned," she announced to Grae once the call ended. "Back for the therapy session." She pushed off the lounge she'd occupied, collected her things, then headed toward the pool house to return the blanket she'd found there.

"Therapy session." Grae shuddered as he followed her. "Why's *that* necessary?"

"Hey, *you're* the one who wanted me to agree to this thing."

"Punch me the next time I come to you with such a great idea."

She laughed and threw Grae a wink over her shoulder. "Do I get to choose where?"

"Depends."

"On?"

"On whether you'll make it feel better once you bruise it."

"Why'd I ask…?"

Grae watched as she put away the blanket, smiling as she stepped onto one of the blackwood ladder-back chairs. Then she was able to reach the cabinet space in the back of the small sitting room area of the cottage.

Thoroughly, he surveyed the area. The stirring bronzed pools of his eyes narrowed.

Tielle was closing the cabinet when she noticed the direction he was heading. Having avoided spending much time in the house in an effort to quell the reminders it evoked, Tielle decided to leave Grae to enjoy his tour alone. She got no farther than the chair she'd used to reach the cabinet when he hooked an arm about her waist.

"New bed?" he asked.

"It is." She masked a feeling of sudden displacement by clearing her throat. "The old one was on its last legs—literally."

"It's nice," Grae said against her temple.

"My guests think so." Tielle took steadying breaths—ones she hoped might settle the rampant beat of her heart. "The summer folks usually like a nap after a swim in the pool or the lake."

"And what about the winter guests?" Grae asked while gently nudging Tielle into the cozy room.

"They love it. Grae, we really should get going to that therapy session."

"What's the rush?" His deep voice was a soothing wave. "It'll take everybody thirty minutes to get there and another thirty to get settled."

"Grae…" His name was little more than a breathy whisper. She attempted to turn in his loose hold at her waist, yet the move wasn't an easy one considering the close quarters and who she was sharing them with.

What remained of her protest segued into a moan when she managed to turn and her tongue became otherwise engaged. Entangled, a ragged, wet kiss commenced between them. Grae quickly tired of aligning his imposing frame to accommodate her slight one. Rising to his full height, he took Tielle with him, keeping her body flush against the chiseled perfection of his.

She launched into resistance mode when her phone buzzed again. "Grae, we don't have time for this."

"We got plenty of time," he argued upon taking a momentary break from stroking his tongue across the roof of her mouth. "My entire family is elsewhere."

"And we should be there, too," Tielle almost purred when he cradled her bottom in his palms while his mouth took a slow glide down her neck and collarbone.

She felt the new bed beneath her back moments later, and Grae settled against her soon after. Eyes closing as though she were delightfully drowsy, Tielle gave in to what she needed from him. Giving in to the pleasure of him there. Tielle worked herself against the erection she'd missed.

Grae set his face next to her clavicle and inhaled. The tender act was fleeting. He needed to see her—*really* see her. Deftly, he pulled her out of her clothes, his lips skimming every silken patch of skin he bared. He lingered near parts of her that he'd missed most dearly, grinning arrogantly when she squirmed against him.

"Grae, we should…go…mmm…you—you told me to tell you to stop…"

He tended to one perky nipple, sheltering the pebble inside skillful lips and bathing it with his tongue. His thumb and forefinger tended to the other. She smiled when she arched more of herself into his mouth.

"Honey, you're not being very convincing," he murmured.

Tielle bit down on her lip to silence a moan. "Listen to my words and not my body." But her words were slurred.

"Are you serious?" He chuckled and continued his erotic journey downward.

Leo blew out a sigh through his end of the phone line. "You let that boy get inside your head, Des. You always do."

"I see. And why, exactly, did you call me today?"

"What Grae said does make me wonder. I'll admit that. The fact that Faro was so hell-bent on having that retreat in that particular venue… Did he say anything else when you saw him this morning?"

"Only what I told you." Desree sighed. "I guess you're right. Letting that child rattle me this way is asinine. He's probably havin' a helluva laugh over it."

"But you don't believe that?" Leo guessed.

"If it is…*that,* how would he know it? He was a boy."

"A clever one, as we both know."

"But if we never spoke on it—"

"There were times," Leo interrupted, "I talked to Ken a lot. He could've overheard."

"But why would he wait until *now* to make an issue of it? I could've understood him doing it six years ago instead of now."

Leo sighed, not wanting further reference to *six years*

ago. Ken Clegg had followed his wife, Grace, into the afterlife.

"Since you called," Des said, "least you can do is give me the benefit of your wisdom. Any suggestions on how to handle this?"

Leo spared a few seconds to send a groan through the line. "The devil with it. Just ask him."

The small pool cottage was quiet except for the sounds of Tielle's hitched cries echoing throughout the three rooms. Her hands were curved into small fists that beat a steady tune against the flexing, ropey muscles of Grae's upper back and shoulders.

He'd relieved her of every scrap of clothing she wore and sent it all to the floor in a graceful tumble. Tielle arched and bucked her hips in a wild fashion until Grae laid a heavy forearm across her belly. The move effectively stifled any movement on Tielle's part.

With her open and settled before him, Grae treated her to a devastating oral display that sent her trembling. Climax stirred within a matter of seconds. Burying all ten fingers in her thick hair, Tielle lost herself in the deeply missed treat. Grae kept his arm across Tielle's belly while his free hand curved over one thigh, tugging it high to improve her position for him.

Tielle's gasping, throaty cries broke through with ease, coaxed by Grae's talented tongue. Her responses livened the air with a continuous stream of sound that, for Grae, was utterly ego-stroking. His head tilted and rotated, slowly at times, then with more fluid speed as he tested some new method of pleasuring her. It all produced the most splendid results, ones that sent Tielle right to the verge of another climax. She could feel herself tipping just slightly over the edge before he tugged her back in a way that possessed a sinful beauty instead of a rugged jarring.

She ordered herself not to beg him. Not wanting to linger in the cottage had little to do with the therapy session they were shamefully late for and everything to do with her not wanting to lower herself to begging him only to be denied again.

"Grae..."

"You want me to stop?"

"No..."

Slowly, he raised his head, easing up over her to tongue her navel with a maddening thoroughness. He charted the sensual course across the undersides of her breasts and the valley between them.

"Tell me what you want me to do, Tielle."

"Take off your clothes," she purred, heart thudding voraciously in her while she kissed herself from his tongue.

Soon, they were both equally bare and loving the feel of being together beyond clothing's boundaries. Sounds of satisfaction stirred from them both. Tielle reveled in the allure of security Grae provided with the power of his magnificent form seductively nudging her body. Each time she attempted pushing him to his back, he bumped the head of his erection against her entrance.

He wasn't of a mind to relinquish a shred of control.

His loose embrace at the base of her throat effectively stilled her into accepting his kiss. He toyed with her tongue, similar to the manner in which he toyed with the rest of her. Frequently, his sex grazed hers, taunting and then denying full pleasure.

Though desperately aroused, Tielle's gasp was prompted mostly by remembrance. "Grae..." Her nails scraped his hips in a subtle sign to have all of him. "Wait…".

"Ti—"

"We need condoms."

Grae's bronzed stare narrowed dangerously. His hand flexed once like a vise on Tielle's hip. He inhaled deeply several times and, while the effort removed a sudden frown, the dangerous glint in his eyes remained.

"You're serious," he said.

"It's okay." She kissed his jaw. "I have plenty."

"You what?" Grae's eyes narrowed almost to the point of closing.

Awareness seized its hold, and Tielle considered his hand at her hip. The hold had taken on a quality less akin to caressing.

"You have condoms."

"Yeah, I—I keep them here. All sizes. I—I know you need larger…" Shrugging, she proffered a weak smile. "It's good to be prepared. I—I never know when the mood might strike my guests."

"Is that right? And what about you?"

She blinked, greater awareness creeping into the cognac orbs of her gaze. "I'm pretty sure you keep a healthy stash somewhere convenient," she challenged, instead of telling him that she hadn't thought about sex with another man in the year they'd been apart. Let alone even seeing someone else.

Grae appeared stunned, almost hurt by the accusation, yet he schooled his expression before it revealed too much. "So is that what you use this place for?"

She shoved at his chest. "Get off me."

"Couldn't even wait for a year, Tel?" He refused to budge. "What about begging me for it last night? Do you keep condoms in the library, too? What would Miss Tina and Miss Danielle think?"

"Wow, Grae, actual questions just spill out when you're angry, don't they?" She gave another shove to the unyielding muscular wall of his chest. "Get off me, dammit! Last night was about me being an idiot for you as usual. It's a good thing you used the head on top of your shoulders then. You so rarely did when we were married."

Her heart seized when he suddenly brought his head in close to trail his nose across her cheek, along her ear…

"I can't recall you ever minding the head I used when we were married, Tel."

Tielle ignored the voice inside her mind and its warning that she not allow her mouth to get her in trouble.

"I so rarely had a choice in the matter," she blurted anyway.

The admission seemed to weaken Grae's resolve. He relieved her of his weight, and Tielle turned her face into the pillow next to the one that had been cradling her head. She watched as he silently went about the task of donning his clothes.

"Grae—" Tielle's words were interrupted by the sight of her clothes being tossed her way courtesy of Graedon.

"You're right, Ti. We're already way too late."

His words made her feel frozen to the bed. She sat there studying the fierce ripple of sinews in his back and shoulders as he jerked his clothes on. She didn't attempt to move until he'd left the cottage. The front door slammed resoundingly behind him.

"We're making a habit of this!" Faro laughed, finding his aunt rounding the long mural-adorned corridor at the same time he did.

Desree's expression was one of playful unease. "Sounds like we're late. Not very commendable."

"Ah, we're good." Faro gave a noncommittal wave. "We're good. It'll take 'em forty-five minutes to get settled anyway."

"That's good, then. It'll give us the chance to talk." Des eased her hands into the side pockets of her denim skirt. "What do you want from me, Faro?"

The pointed question only roused sudden laughter from the man.

"You already told me—what was it again? A few more get-togethers might give me an idea of how I could spare the family more drama. Drama about what?"

"Des, come on." Faro's resulting grin was not a humorous one. "Stop playing the clueless role. You can't pull it off."

"Drama about what?"

Faro sighed, studying his hands as he rubbed them together. "Since discussing all the particulars understandably makes me want to vomit, let's just say it's drama about a little...what was the word they used to use for it? Issue?"

Desree gasped. "How—" She stopped herself, realizing that the question would only solidify what Faro thought—and what she *knew*—to be fact.

"What do you want from me?" she asked instead.

Satisfaction smoothed the harsh lines in Faro's angular face. "One of two things my father left to others that should've been mine."

"Your father was a smart man." Understanding gleamed on Desree's lovely face. "He knew his business wouldn't survive a year with you at the helm."

"That's what he thought—" Faro shrugged beneath

a silk dress shirt "—but as we both know, he wasn't really the best judge of character."

Desree was close enough to slap her nephew, and she did. The blow echoed in the corridor despite the voices of family members resonating beyond the living room where the therapy session would soon be underway.

"Why would you do this now?" she hissed.

"I could've done it earlier if not for momentary weakness," Faro sneered, touching the back of his hand to where Desree's blow had landed. "I actually believed my ex-sister-in-law might really pull off the trick of getting my perfect little brother to go against Daddy's wishes for once in his life. She might've managed to do it, too, if Grae didn't hate me so much."

"Such emotions aren't one-sided, you know? They only come into play as defense mechanisms."

"That's right." Faro smiled at the argument. "Always an excuse for Grae. Is that because he's the baby?"

"Why do you want that deed, Faro?"

"Grae's already got the building. I at least deserve the land—*some* part of Dad's legacy. He was my father, too, right, Des?"

"Don't play the loving-son role with me, Faro. It's impossible for you to pull that off." Des turned her nephew's earlier jibe around on him. "Ken gave you no part of his legacy for a reason. I'd betray his memory if I did."

"Right...memories." Faro nodded and began a short stroll of the corridor. "Some are powerful—impossible—to file away once they're in your head. You know what I like best about memories though, Des?" He looked her way then. "Sharing them. It's something I have no qualms about doing."

Desree merely turned her back on Faro and headed into the living room. Faro wasn't far behind. Neither noticed Grae watching them from down the long hall.

Chapter 8

The Clegg family therapy session was already set to be a stress-filled affair without the pressure of a lover's spat perched on top of the pile. Yet Tielle ordered herself to withstand the agitation as she rounded the corner and went down the corridor leading to the living room selected for the gathering.

She felt a few layers of her apprehension lift when she spotted Desree. Unfortunately, that brief relief dissolved when her assessing stare met Grae's stony one. He sat in one of the wide maroon armchairs in the alcove. The choice of seating put a noticeable distance between him and the rest of his family. The others had selected seating on the sofas, love seats and other cushioned chairs that the staff had arranged more to the center of the room.

Figuring Grae's request that she remain by his side during the retreat's events was then null and void, Tielle opted for the settee near the room's entrance.

"You're welcome to move closer, Ti." Dr. Valerie DeLoache's voice held subtle amusement.

Tielle appeared to shudder over the suggestion. "Please don't make me." She lowered her head.

Dr. DeLoache twittered a laugh before patting her boss's shoulder and moving on into the living area to greet the Clegg group.

* * *

"…I spent ten years on staff there, before leaving Chicago to join Ms. Turner's organization. I've been the retreat's lead therapist for the past five years," Valerie DeLoache told the group as they settled in for the session.

"In addition to welcoming you all to our beautiful estate, I'd also like to commend your family for acting proactively to fix the issues causing whatever tensions exist among you—"

"Thank you, Dr. DeLoache," Asia called out before the woman could continue, "but I think many of us here would agree that there's nothing causing tension in our family…anymore."

With that said, most heads in the room turned toward Tielle. She commanded her eyes to remain fixed on the colorful landscaped piece above the fireplace mantle.

"That's a close-minded perspective, Asia," Faro told his cousin before the doctor could respond. "Tielle only tried to get us to own up to issues we had long before she ever became one of us."

"She was *never* one of us," Asia retorted.

"Cut it out, girl," admonished one of the uncles.

"She tried to help us," Faro said. "That was until she had the will to do so stifled by bullying and ultimatums."

"Mr. Clegg, I'm sure—"

The doctor's words were then interrupted by Grae's rumbling voice. "Something you need to say to me, Faro?"

"There's a lot I need to *say to you*." Faro refused to look at his brother.

Grae spread his hands. "Well? Let's have it."

"You see, Doctor?" Asia cried. "They never griped like this before she came along."

"Asia, shut it!" Ranata ordered through clenched teeth.

Stunned by her usually calm-natured cousin, Asia piped up to rake the woman over the coals.

"Your instigating and snide remarks caused just as much trouble for Grae and Ti as Grae did with his bullying," Asia said before her cousin could blast her. "All that foolishness from Grae is what lost him Tielle, leaving us to deal with the ogre he's become."

"Ladies." Valerie remained professional, admirably calm despite the ripple of tension Asia's remark sent through the room. "This is a wonderful start. You guys are venting and giving voice to your feelings, but we need to do it in a more constructive—"

"You two hush," Barry ordered the bickering cousins. "Grae's got every right to be pissed about what went on back then. His only fault was comin' down so hard on Tielle when it was Faro who deserved to be kicked in the teeth."

"These young folk in the family are a mess," Jill agreed with her brother.

"Amen." Paul sighed.

Tielle bowed her head and battled the urge to up and leave the room. Resolute, she looked up to catch Desree's gaze. *The woman appears defeated,* Tielle thought, watching as Des shook her head once in regret.

The living room swelled with the volume of voices chiming in on the subject then.

"Everyone—" Dr. DeLoache stood, waving her hands for calm, and was completely overlooked.

"Uncle Barry, you and Uncle Paul should shut up," Asia spat. "All you focus on when you see Tielle are her tits and ass, so excuse me if your opinions mean squat."

"Guys, please."

Quiet settled, and it seemed that the therapist had finally gained control of her wayward group. In reality, the control had more to do with the fact that everyone had stopped arguing to catch their breaths.

"People, nothing will be settled until you all allow one another the time and courtesy to hear each other."

"No, Doc," Faro intervened. "Nothing will be settled until these people admit that all the *mess*—" he stressed the word while sending his aunt Jill a pointed look "—started with the older folks protecting a lot of dirty secrets that got all the mistrust started in the first place."

"Not this again," his cousin, Wendell Clegg, groaned. "Faro, what in the *hell* are you talkin' about?"

"I'm willin' to bet there are those who really don't know, but there're even more who do and they've kept it quiet for way too long," Faro insisted.

"I need to talk to you, Faro," Desree announced as she suddenly got to her feet.

Dr. DeLoache rushed forward. "Ms. Clegg—"

"Alone!"

"Des—"

"Now, Faro!"

Jaws dropped as the usually poised and cool-natured Desree blustered past her family on her way out of the living room. Despite his earlier boldness, even Faro appeared rather unnerved by his aunt's summons.

Tielle gave none of her former in-laws the benefit of her gaze. She was too busy studying Grae's expression. He remained in his remote corner not looking at his family but hunched over in his chair. His elbows were braced on his knees while he used one hand to stroke his jaw. Tielle thought he reflected an element of true concentration...and suspicion. She could hear the murmur of voices easing in as the group tried to make sense of what had just happened. She took advantage of the confusion to make her escape.

It was as though he'd sensed her intentions before she had the chance to put them into action. Tielle saw Grae slide his extraordinary stare her way. He watched her with the same mix of concentration and suspicion. The look was enough to make Tielle shred the last of her procrastination and leave the room.

"Tielle, wait up!"

Valerie's call sent a thread of resentment sliding along Tielle's spine. Still, she lost some of her edginess when she turned to face the woman. Tielle could see that the normally unflustered doctor was then looking decidedly rattled around the edges.

"Need a drink, Val?" Tielle teased.

The woman tucked a lock of chestnut-brown hair behind her ear and risked a glance across her shoulder. Most of the group was still embroiled in heated debate.

"What is it with them?" she asked. "Everyone wants to be heard, no one wants to listen."

Tielle studied her ex in-laws for a moment, as well. "You've just given a perfect definition of the Clegg family."

"Any advice on how you managed to get a word in with them?"

"Well," Tielle indulged in a playful smile, "talking with the Cleggs wasn't really my top priority when I was married to Grae."

Valerie's expression took on the same playful tint then. The tall brunette cast a knowing and understatedly sultry smile toward Grae, who still occupied his seat across the room. "Understood." She gave her boss a nod and then regarded the rest of the family. "You think they might be up for another session?"

Tielle gave a woeful grin. "My guess is that it won't be today."

Valerie nodded toward the room's entrance. "Any thoughts on what the rest is about between the aunt and nephew?"

Tielle resisted the urge to look over at Grae. "Whatever it is, it's nothing good."

"So your scheme to get the family here for repair was really about ripping it apart."

"I love my family, Des." Faro touched a hand to his chest while voicing the declaration. "I'm not interested in ripping it apart, only in ripping out lies."

"I see..." Desree observed him with her arms folded and lips parted in disdain. "And how did you come by these...lies?"

"Kids are told to be seen and not heard. Adults never tell them they aren't supposed to listen."

"You always were a foul child." Desree shook her head. "But I never would've thought you were capable of something so evil."

"So telling the truth is evil now, Des?"

"What purpose will doing this serve?"

"The same purpose that you signing over that deed will serve."

An understanding smile illuminated Desree's plump face. "So *that's* what you want."

Faro's mouth thinned into a belligerent line. "It should've been mine anyway."

"There was a reason why your father didn't leave it to you. He knew you were unworthy."

"Well, it doesn't matter now, does it? He's gone."

"Grae will never—"

"Grae's days on the throne are numbered, Des. Maybe it's time you put your trust in another."

"Sweetie, you're getting me mixed up with whoever is idiotic enough to be afraid of you."

Menace further shaded Faro's dark stare. "You'd do well to be afraid. I have no qualms about doing what I have to."

"And you'd do it here, of all places?" Again, Desree grimaced. "Tielle was one of the few people who believed in you. She bet her marriage on it. You'd actually let her see it was all for nothing?"

Faro waved his hand to the side. "Grae's insecurity busted up his marriage, and I'm sick of being blamed for it. Maybe once he's relieved of the responsibility of running Dad's business, he'll have the time he needs to get his wife back."

"Little bastard—"

"Tsk, tsk, Des. Do you really want to take the conversation there?"

"I don't have the deed with me."

"Ah...good. You've seen the light." Faro's gleeful expression merged into a glare. "I believe Leo has your power of attorney. He should be able to collect it from the safety deposit box at your bank with no trouble."

Desree's gasp reinstated Faro's gleeful expression.

"My ears have served me well over the years."

"Oh, and I'd love to box them for you."

Faro's laughter was fleeting. "Call Leo and have him get the deed here no later than Friday."

"That's two days away! Why would you want to carry on this charade?"

"Well, Des, there's not much reason for you to stick to your part of the deal if I have nothing to bargain with." He moved in close. "Get the deed or the next family therapy session we have won't end with me being ordered to follow you from the room like a hardheaded child, but with you being left to answer a lot of questions and kiss a lot of wounds."

He looked thoughtful. "On second thought, kissing wounds may not be involved. I'm pretty sure certain parties will be way too devastated to accept kisses from the ones who betrayed them." He brushed past Des. "Two days," he called.

"Oh...sorry I..." Tielle muttered, having rounded the corner of the terrace to find Grae alone and seated on one of the lounges. He stared out past the terrace railing toward the dense brush and trees beyond the rear lawn. Tielle decided to take her leave.

"Do you remember this place?" he asked. "First time we were out here after we got married?"

Slowly, Tielle ventured farther onto the terrace. She loved it there—the majesty of the trees already half through their annual shedding of leaves. The wind held a thriving intensity that afternoon that promised to strip the remaining foliage from its branches before nightfall.

"I remember." Memories of their wedding reception shifted to the front of her mind. "It was too cold and everybody went back inside."

Grae bowed his head, smiling. "Didn't feel cold to me."

"Probably because we were curled up on one of those lounges."

"Humph. We didn't stay there for long."

Tielle shook her head. Her gaze fixed as though she

were viewing a replay of the scene. "We had our first dance out here...then it started to snow. We didn't even notice it or that everybody came to the doors to watch us."

"Photographers snapping tons of pictures..." Grae laughed. "We only noticed because it'd gotten dark and the flash bothered us."

"Ha! Yeah, one of your dad's cousins said he'd never seen lightning during a blizzard."

Grae's rich laughter seemed to echo. "His wife, Miranda, told him only someone as drunk as him could see that."

"They aren't here for the retreat," Tielle noted once she and Grae had a long laugh at the couple's expense. "Are they okay?"

"Hugh's had some close calls—heart, liver...Miranda decided they'd sit this trip out. She said it was the first time Hugh's rotten liver had done her any good and that being around this bunch for a week was a treat she'd had more than enough of."

"I always liked them." Tielle dissolved into more laughter and used the oversized cuff of her knit sweater to dab a tear from her eye. "Guess there're quite a few of your family wishing they'd made another decision about coming here."

"Including you?" Grae turned his head but didn't make eye contact with her. "Guess I should apologize for asking you to accept Faro's request to bring us up here."

Tielle paced a short path on the terrace. "If being here helps someone get closure, then I guess it's all worth it."

"Humph...closure...I've always wondered about that word." He looked at her. "Whatever can of worms my brother wants to open won't give anyone closure. It'd just be another load of drama we'll all have to deal with."

"At least it'll be dealt with, right?"

He smiled. "You think it's that easy to *deal* with things?"

She gave a lazy shrug. "If all parties are willing to work at it, not just draw lines in the sand."

"Humph. Parties like me, huh?"

"Grae, I didn't—"

"Who is he?"

The question, as out of place as it was unexpected, rendered Tielle quiet for a time. "Grae—"

"How long was it before you let him in your bed, Tel?"

"How long before one of your scores of admirers was in *your* bed?" she countered hotly.

Graedon turned on the lounge, giving Tielle the full benefit of an ambivalent glare. "Getting back at me for something you *think* I'm doing, Tel? You never played the assumption game before."

"There's a lot I never did before."

"Like asking me to use a condom."

"Please." Her eyes narrowed to lovely slits. "Do not sit there and act like you've got *no* clue why I'd ask that. I'm sure the offers to warm your bed started to roll in before you wrote the last *G* in *Clegg* when you signed our divorce papers."

"The offers never *stopped* rolling in, Tel," he growled. "They were persistent, something I got every day of our marriage."

She smiled. "How nice it must be that you don't have it in your way anymore."

"Neither do you."

"Grae…" She closed her eyes, standing still and counting for calm. "We don't need to be doing this. You're handling enough drama in your family without creating more between the two of us."

"Creating?"

Tielle threw up her hands. "The terrace is all yours."

Grae pushed off the lounge. Going to the railing, he folded his hands over the wrought iron and squeezed. He prayed for restraint, commanding himself to listen to the voice that told him not to follow Tielle's departure but to let their budding disagreement die. The voice failed in its task.

"To hell with it," he muttered and bolted a heated path from the terrace.

Tielle resisted the urge to slam her bedroom door when she beat a clear trail there from the terrace. She tossed down the work she'd intended to handle and watched the folders, pads and her tablet slide across the wide antique pine desk in the corner.

She stood in the middle of the room with her hands on her hips. In fewer than twenty seconds, she dissolved into a puddle of laughter. The argument with her ex and how it all started was the catalyst for her amusement. She dropped to the bed and was still laughing when Grae barreled into the room.

Finding his ex-wife overwhelmed by laughter diminished whatever argument he'd come to deliver.

"I'm sorry, Tel," his said in one rush of breath. "It's none of my business who you see or—or sleep with—"

He swallowed back something distasteful that followed those words. "Even so, I won't lie and tell you it doesn't piss the hell out of me to even think about it."

His words had a sobering effect on Tielle. "There's no one else, Grae." She shook her head. "Not only don't I have the time, but I've got no desire for any other man. Humph. I'm an unbelievable idiot for telling you this, but you're kind of a hard act to follow."

He gaped at her. "And you think you're not?"

"Not sure." Tielle's cognac gaze faltered, and she studied the bed comforter's elaborate stitching. "It seemed pretty easy for you to walk away from me before."

"Easy? You thought that was easy, Tel."

He stated the last as fact, and Tielle could see the upset filtering his stirring gaze. "Grae," she said, scooting to the bed's edge, "we shouldn't talk about this now, not after the day we've had."

Hurt pooled his expression. "You really think I'm that much of a pig that I could have another woman warming your place in my bed just like that?" He followed the declaration with a snap of his fingers.

"Grae, I'm sorry." She left the bed. "I shouldn't have said that."

"Damn straight you shouldn't have."

His words had reclaimed their growling intensity. He looked totally unapproachable, yet Tielle remained undaunted.

"You need to calm down. It's been a crazy day." She ran her hands over the chorded bulges of his arms defined beneath the sweatshirt he wore.

"It's been a crazy day…" she soothed as much for his benefit as hers.

Tielle thought she was making headway given the change in his expression. She discovered that she'd completely misread him when he captured her upper arms. Effortlessly, he took her off her feet, settling her flush against him so that they were eye to eye.

Again, Tielle realized she'd mistaken his mood. The steadiness of his glare screamed *hostile*.

"Grae—" His name was the last word she was allowed to utter before her tongue was otherwise engaged. He occupied her mouth in an act of seeking exploration, bruising and sensual in its intensity.

Tielle may have criticized herself for the whimpering moans that escaped her lips were she not so terribly in need of what he was giving her. Languidly, she drew her legs up around his hips while simultaneously winding her arms up over his shoulders and locking her hands about his neck.

Grae's moves didn't harbor the same fluidity. Need for her overruled any possibility for finesse. He was of the single-minded intention to take her to his content. His tongue filled her mouth with a force that could have snapped her neck, but she met it with equal heat. Grae treated her to an array of potent lunges before dragging kisses of similar intensity down her throat. He paused to infrequently gnaw the supple flesh of her shoulders and the base of her throat. The V-necked cashmere slipped and shifted as Grae went on, exposing more of her skin. The loose material revealed the silk cami she wore beneath.

Keeping her sealed against him, Grae still managed to disrobe her, peeling away the delicate undershirt. His strong teeth against her flesh was soothed with a gentle bath from his tongue.

Tielle felt the bed against her back for only a moment before Grae put her on her stomach. He finished freeing her of the cami. The gravelly tones originating from his chest caused a shiver to rush along Tielle's spine, yet she craved to be free of her clothes.

Grae's thinking ran along the same lines. Impatient to have her bare to his gaze, he pushed his hand beneath her belly to expertly undo the button fastening on her jeans. Once he'd freed it, Grae didn't tug the jeans down her legs. Instead, he slipped a hand between the zipper's teeth, easing his hungry fingers along the dampening crotch of her panties when she shifted to open herself to him.

"Grae..." His name sounded ragged when she spoke it into the pillow cradling her cheek. Her sharp gasp accompanied the slight tear he made in her panties as he pushed her thighs farther open to accept his fingers inside the lacy undergarment.

Tielle moaned his name again.

That time, Grae covered her with his weight. He cupped her jaw, angling her head to kiss her again. Tielle raised her head a bit to improve their positioning. She went weak all over, unable even to thrust her tongue with any real effort. His middle finger ceased its tormenting rubs up and down the dark caramel-toned petals of her sex and plundered beyond.

Her persistent moans of his name held no volume behind the word. Grae steadily explored her mouth, his tongue tangling with hers before charting a journey across the ridge of her teeth. He tasted the roof of her mouth, reengaging her tongue when she hiccupped a gasp.

Grae's fingers played a scandalous melody upon her body. Eventually, Tielle was so drugged with sensation that she could no longer take part in the erotic dance between their tongues. She rested her head on the pillows and gave herself over to the delight his touch drummed inside her. Shamelessly wanton, she moved with an alluring grace upon the covers, tangling them beneath her body.

"Grae please…more…" she begged until he had her totally naked.

"More what?"

Tielle smiled at the actual question he'd managed. "Everything," she moaned.

"Specifics, please." He drove his middle finger high and rotated it slowly.

"Mmm…th-that…"

"Just like that?"

"More…Grae…please…" she whined when he stilled his finger. "More fingers," she urged, nudging her bare frame into his massive one, which smothered her in the most delicious way. "Take off your clothes…"

He chuckled. "You've got me a little busy right now." He'd added his index and ring finger to the X-rated massage.

Tielle ended her begging and accepted the ecstasy claiming her. Her gasping breaths and low moans were meant to encourage Grae. She didn't want him to stop until she'd achieved every bit of her satisfaction.

Grae unraveled the French braid she wore, needing to feel the coarse beauty of her hair between his fingers. The sound of her hitched cries and panting ushered in a hint of jealousy from Grae. He wanted to experience more of the joy she was capable of giving him.

With hungry determination, he dragged his mouth across her skin while jerking out of his clothes. He took his mouth off her only to pull his sweatshirt over his head. He worked his tongue between her shoulder blades while kicking out of his boots, socks, jeans and boxers.

Tielle luxuriated atop the covers; a messy tangle then. She caught the edge of a pillowcase between her teeth, hoping to silence the gurgle of her delighted screams. He was tonguing the small of her back and at the same time encircling her hips to apply a dual-thumb massage to her center.

"Grae, no…"

He deprived her of his touch, putting her on her back. She complained until the feel of condom packets sprinkling her tummy sent laughter tickling her throat.

"All for me?" she asked.

"Only you," he confirmed, covering her body with his and gently nuzzling his tongue into her mouth. There, he began a kiss that transitioned from sweet to lusty in the space of a heartbeat. Her small, ravenous whimpers had him muttering curses in criticism of his hands. They were shaking from need and anticipation.

Grae managed to ease the erratic movements by clenching his fists. Winning the battle over the shaking allowed him to apply their protection.

Tielle kept her fingers clenched in the glossy mass of curls covering his head. A surprised and smothered grunt mingled into the kiss they shared when the wide head of his shaft teased her entrance.

With maddening slowness, Grae invaded, stretching and spreading her as he overwhelmed, filled and pleasured. Tielle's hands slid from the dark cloud of his hair to fist against his broad pecs.

"Grae it—it's been a year," she reminded him.

Arrogant awareness defined the already alluring curve of his mouth. "Yes, it has." He had no complaints about the wet, tight sheath steadily enveloping his sex. Keeping her thighs wide for him, he nuzzled the softness below her ear and eased himself home.

Tielle felt deliciously suspended between pleasure and tension. She trembled, but there was no escaping his hold, not that she would've dreamed of doing anything so foolish. The low, indecipherable sounds of need that he emitted just beneath her ear kept her in a state of disbelief that she'd done without him for so long.

Grae continued to fill her until he was completely buried inside her. Tielle felt her toes flex when he moved, stirring her slowly, working her into an erotic frenzy. He exhaled slow, satisfied breaths into her neck as she gloved him in a deep, drenched haven from which he never wanted to leave.

Tielle felt the throb of tension lessen the longer Grae subjected her to his probing drives. They succeeded in stretching her to accommodate his size more appropriately. Whatever doubts her ex may've had about how… active…she'd been during their year apart, they had to be settled.

Grae could get his mind to formulate little in the way of cohesive thought. Tielle was still miraculously tight despite his stretching power. Then again, she'd always fit him like a tailor-made glove. The acknowledgment set a ragged sound building in his chest, and his seed erupted inside the condom's thin sheeting moments later.

Almost instantly, Grae refueled for another round of love. Tielle's heart thudded out a frantic, elated beat in anticipation for what more was to come.

Chapter 9

"Coming!"

Tielle made no move to leave the bed. Smiling, she wondered at how many times she'd cried out that word during the night before and into the wee hours of the morning. Sadly, the context in which she had just used the word didn't hold quite the same punch of delight.

Unfortunately, the person carrying out the insistent stream of knocking on her bedroom door clearly had no sympathy for the hour of the day.

"Are you in there?"

Tielle lifted her head from the pillow when she heard Laura's voice. At least the voice *sounded* like Laura's but was far removed from her usual easy tone. The woman on the other side of the door sounded...panicked.

"Laura?" Cautious, Tielle pushed back the covers with every intention of racing for the door. Then, her body reminded her of what she'd been doing the night before.

"Coming," Tielle called again, her voice more strained and less drowsy that time. Tielle reached for the sheet that was virtually free of the bed with the exception of the corner barely tucked beneath the mattress. She wrapped herself in it on the way to the door.

Laura quieted once the door opened, and she studied Tielle on the other side of it. She opened her mouth, closed it and then tilted her head at a curious angle. "You okay?" she asked.

"Fantastic." Tielle clutched the sheet tighter about her otherwise nude body and appeared wholly honest. She waved Laura inside. "What's up?"

"There's a—" Laura paused, taking in the sight of the bedroom. She then shifted another measuring glance in Tielle's direction. "What happened in here?"

Tielle leaned on the door, closing it in the process, and rested herself against it. "Everything." She sighed.

Laura arched a brow. "Obviously." She noted a torn lace cami that had somehow hooked itself on the doorknob.

Tielle gave a little wince. "You mind if we don't discuss it?"

"You might prefer to once I tell you why I'm here."

The foreboding words sent Tielle bracing off the door. "What?" Weariness cleared her expression to make way for mounting unease.

"There's press out front."

"What? Why? How?" Tielle fired the questions while slowly closing the distance between her and Laura.

"The *what* is there's press out front. The *why* is I don't know, and from what I gathered from the members of the media I encountered when I asked what they were doing at our front gates, the *how* is because your brother-in-law called them."

Tielle closed her eyes against the pressure of despair. "What's he done?" she moaned.

"Well, no one's seen him yet this morning, so…"

Tielle ran a hand through her wild hair, grabbed a

fistful and gave it a yank. "Did they tell you anything else? The press?"

"They said he told them he had an announcement to make."

"And he wants the press there for it...great..." Tielle rubbed at her temples. "Has anyone else in the house gotten wind of it yet?"

"You mean besides the house staff?" Laura sighed. "Only the entire Clegg family in residence. Maybe with the exception of Grae. No one's seen him this morning, either." She favored Tielle with another interested look. "The rest of the family is already heading to breakfast in the terrace dining room."

Tielle made a beeline for her closet.

"We can't afford having the press out there like that."

"Well, what do you suggest, Laura? Inviting them in for breakfast?" Tielle snapped from the bowels of her closet then made her way out to face Laura. "I'm sorry."

"*I* should be apologizing." Laura waved a hand. "Looks like something pretty amazing happened in here last night."

"Yeah..." The observation took the edge off a great deal of Tielle's anxiety. "It did...but we've got work to do. Starting with giving the Cleggs the best breakfast they've ever had and keeping them out of sight from the press."

"On it." Laura headed for the room's door, but hesitated before opening it. "Maybe after all this is done, you and Grae can get lost for a few days, huh?"

"Get out," Tielle ordered, though the smile on her face proved what an excellent idea she thought it was.

Laura left her with a wink, and Tielle continued her trek toward the closet. She paused for another look around the room, paying particular attention to the disarrayed bed. She smiled. Things were still a mess between her and Grae, probably more so in light of whatever Faro was brewing.

She shook her head, not wanting to wrap herself up in the hope that a chance was on the horizon. Still, she couldn't resist praying that one was. She smoothed her hands over her arms when a shiver of anticipation kissed her skin. A wince followed the motion, the pressure from her hands agitating the bruise above the bend of her elbow.

Her smile returned, and Tielle wondered how many scratches her ex was wearing on his back that morning. Suggestive tingles attacked her someplace intimate, and Tielle left off her daydreaming to prepare for another day of Clegg fireworks.

Grae didn't bother with catching a few extra hours of sleep once he'd returned from Tielle's room that night— well, that morning. He was way too wired, despite how thoroughly, how impressively, he'd been depleted. He'd taken her over every square inch of that way-too-neat bedroom of hers.

Smirking, Grae recalled the state in which he'd left the room. Quickly, he closed his eyes to shut down the memory that threatened to return him to the state of almost throbbing arousal he'd endured since spending a full day in his ex-wife's presence after a year of separation.

Ex-wife…

He grumbled a silent obscenity over the phrase. That was a status long overdue to be changed, but when, dammit? Grae tossed aside the damp hand towel he'd been using to dry his hair following a long shower.

He'd expected Faro to have already revealed all or at

least some of the hand he was using to play his game of Family Secrets and Lies, but the man had been remarkably cool. The longer he remained so, Grae knew the longer he'd have to wait to devote his full attention to Tielle. The longer it would take to bring her home where she belonged.

Grae closed off the thoughts that would only fuel his anger. He reached for the hand towel and ran it through still-damp hair. He was tugging at the knot securing the bath towel at his hips when a knock fell to his room door. Unmindful of appearance, he answered.

"Tel." His rough voice was whisper soft when he saw her.

Tielle's purpose for the trip down to Grae's guest suite flew right out of her mind. She could feel her mouth hanging open but had no inclination to shut it. In helpless fascination, her gaze traced the heat-inducing ripple and flex of his chest, broad and perfectly defined. This reaction, despite the fact that she'd just had the pleasure of the chiseled plane beneath her fingertips, against her back and thighs, as they'd pleasured each other in the most explicit ways.

She heard a gasp and realized that it had thankfully not come from her, but one of the upstairs room attendants. The young woman had caught sight of Grae and stood rooted to her spot. The fresh linens she carried promised a tumble to the floor while she ogled the half-dressed male in the doorway.

"Morning, Chelsie," Tielle said while pushing Grae into the room and closing the door behind them.

"Sorry about that," he said.

"Sure you are." She risked another indulgent scan of his body. "I see you're not out and about yet."

"Getting a late start. You completely exhausted me."

"Sure I did."

Grae indulged in his own survey of his wife's attire. Slowly, his cool bronze eyes studied the subtly alluring cut of the peach wrap dress she wore. "I see you're up and at 'em. You know I could probably use another shower if you'd like to join me."

"Be serious."

"I am."

Tielle took note of their position then. Grae had not put much distance between them since she had pushed him back into the room. Sandwiched between him and the door was perhaps not the best place to be if she'd come there for discussion and...nothing more.

"There're reporters outside. Faro arranged for them to be here."

"Wonder what that's about?" Grae's consideration of the issue was scant.

He rested a shoulder against the door. Tielle clenched her fists to resist running her hand across the sleek, honey-toned surface of his magnificent chest. She cleared her throat when he noticed her staring.

"I, um, I came down—came by—because I didn't want you to get...agitated..." Her eyes traveled helplessly downward.

"I'm not agitated, Tel. I only want Faro to make his point so we can get this over with and I can focus on why I came down here."

"You came down here for your family."

"*You're* my family."

"Grae, we need to get downstairs." He was dipping his

head to kiss her. "Everybody's on edge—" She moaned as his tongue drew hers into an erotic dance. "Reporters are at the front door," she managed when he broke the kiss. "Faro hasn't come down yet."

"Good, that gives us time…"

"We have no time." She made half fists against his chest when he launched an assault on her earlobe. "They're already asking for you."

"They can keep asking."

"Grae…" His name slid into a moan from her tongue. His fingers had found the side entrance provided by the design of her dress.

Grae was skirting her thigh, celebrating that panties were all she wore beneath the frock. The garment made a quick trip to the floor after a few insistent tugs. His tongue coaxed her lips apart while his fingers made their presence known. Relentlessly, they plundered her core, instantly reducing the spot to a quivering, moist mass. The kiss he requested deepened when his middle finger probed high.

He treated her to an exchange of thrusts and rotations that put Tielle on the toes of her platform pumps. She wanted to experience every nuance of his touch. Her kiss held a shameless desperation and carried with it unsteady moans with each scrape of her tongue against his.

Her heart flew into her throat when he suddenly hoisted her high, bringing her to his eye level. Setting her back against the door, he secured her there with a knee between her thighs.

"Grae…" His name was a warning veiled within a caress.

Tielle felt the unmistakable bump of an insistent erection, and she pushed at his shoulders with more warning.

Grae didn't argue, simply kept her close, gnawing at her neck before pampering the ravaged space beneath his tongue. He held her easily with one arm banded about her waist. She realized he was taking her deeper into the room.

Although there were more pressing things needing to be handled, Tielle could summon interest only in what was happening at that moment. She wanted it. It was *all* she wanted. She'd let herself surrender to the mastery of Graedon Clegg's touch, to indulge herself.

Disappointment sidled in, however, when Grae slowed his steps toward the bed, which she thought—hoped— was his intended destination. He stopped at the bureau and slanted a wink her way. Tielle realized he was rummaging around in the top drawer for the condoms. She smiled, hiding her face against his neck while he elbowed the drawer shut.

Tielle renewed her anticipation of being carried to the bed, but Grae had other plans. She found herself against the wall next to the bureau, and she was once more secured by his wide length. Blinking madly, she relished the sensation of his expansive cylinder of muscle stimulating her sex.

Cupping her thighs, Grae plied her with a teasing kiss that invited Tielle to chase his tongue and slowly suckle it when she emerged victorious. Her low, satisfied purrs as they kissed motivated Grae to come out of the bath towel that was then only loosely knotted at his trim waist.

Grae didn't need to ensure that she was wet enough to take him easily. He could feel her need dousing his thigh where it was snugly lodged against the part of her that he ached for—was rock hard and throbbing for.

Tielle's purr transitioned into a quivering moan when she heard the foil packet rattle as he ripped into it with his perfect teeth. With protection handled, he claimed her in a swift, filling lunge that forced her to sob out a breath. The folds of her peach wrap dress flowed gorgeously about her bared thighs cradled in Grae's hands as he positioned them high about his hips.

She wanted to urge him on, to beg him not to stop or change a thing he was doing to her. She had no words—none she could articulate at the moment, anyway. Grae kept his head bowed while he worked her body to his satisfaction.

The sight of her sheathing his sex inside hers and the creamy need coating his shaft when he withdrew made Grae's pulse thrive. The intensity was so shattering, he swore he could feel the blood zipping through his veins.

He put his head on her shoulder and listened to her sex-driven cries that stoked his ego and desire. He was sensitive enough to feel her walls tensing beautifully around him.

Tielle came violently around the lengthy pleasure-inducing organ as it continued to pummel her with sensational thrusts that stretched her deliciously. She felt a definite sense of emptiness when he retreated. Her toes flexed inside the confines of her suede heels when he went even more rigid inside her only seconds before his seed poured heavily into the condom.

Grae squeezed her bottom, dragging a ragged kiss across her neck as she milked him of all he had to give. Then, he was drawing her earlobe between his teeth. "Take a shower with me?"

"Grae…" Tielle spread her hands across his chest,

but couldn't summon power to press against it. "No… we need to be downstairs."

"No…*I* need to be right where I am." He took a moment or three, inhaling deeply before pulling away from the wall and taking her with him.

"I can get another shower in my room."

"It'll be more fun with me…"

Smoothing her hands across the magnificent ridges of his shoulders, she let her gaze soften with the love she still had for him. She studied his damp hair smattered across his head in wavy ringlets. Drops of water glistened in his close-cut beard to present an irresistible combination. It solidified Tielle's certainty that if she gave in to one more request, they'd be indisposed for the rest of the day.

"Grae, this is my business," she said to him in the language of entrepreneurship, hoping it would penetrate the erotic haze through which he was operating. "Reporters at a business like mine could cause a lot of panic that I can't afford."

Silently, Grae could admit that he wanted the reporters to do their worst. Her business dissolving would leave her free to come back to him, right? The more rational side of him triumphed, however, encouraging him to let her go but not before he backed her against another wall. He treated Tielle to a kiss that coaxed her to toss her earlier cautions right out the door. Her moan was a mix of delight and disappointment when she realized he was allowing her to slide down the length of the wall.

"It'd be best for you not to find yourself alone with me again today if you plan on focusing on your business," he advised.

"Understood." She cast a fleeting look around the room.

"Good." He gave a caressing squeeze to her upper arm.

The brief pump around her arm was enough to initiate a wince from Tielle. Her reaction was faint but enough to draw attention.

Grae cocked his head inquisitively. "What?"

"Grae—"

"Did I hurt you? Was it last night? Just now?"

"It's fine, Grae—"

"Dammit, Tel." He bowed his head, grinding down hard while his jaw muscle flexed. "Please don't give me that lie when—" he pumped her arm again and grimaced at her wince "—I can see proof that you're not."

"Please listen to me." Keeping her expression cool, she patted his bare chest in a reassuring fashion. "I'm all right. You didn't hurt me it—it's just an aftereffect."

"Aftereffect." He repeated the word as though it was obscene.

"Just please get downstairs." Tielle was too preoccupied by that morning's goings-on to spend added time soothing Grae's concerns. She kissed his cheek and left him with a smile that was not reciprocated.

Chapter 10

"Where's Faro?"

"Where's Grae?"

The two questions were bandied about in the midst of conversation regarding the slew of reporters at the gates of Turner Estates and Gardens. While the main gates couldn't be seen from the house, a morning golf game between a few early rising of the family revealed the media presence. Some of the craftier members of the press found their way on the property by taking the long way around to the course where they proceeded to ask the golfers a few choice questions.

"What's all this about new management?"

"Why don't *we* know about it?"

"What will your stockholders do when they ask why *they* didn't know about it?"

"Where's Faro?"

"Good question," Tielle said to Laura after they arrived in the dining room and caught remnants of the various conversations.

"How'd all this get traced back to Faro anyway?" Tielle warmed her hands over the cashmere sleeves of the sweater she'd changed into after her second shower.

"Apparently the press who talked with the family this

morning told them Faro had an important announcement to make, so they just threw in some of their own assumptions."

"And since he's yet to make an appearance…" Tielle raised her eyebrows.

Laura reciprocated the gesture. "Right…What do we do, Ti?"

Tielle massaged a mounting ache near her temple. "What else? Go into the lion's den and try to calm the lions."

"Faro!" Someone saw the man entering the room, and the din of conversation raised several decibels.

"He looks calm," Laura softly noted.

Tielle wasn't convinced. "Yeah…calm."

"Everyone, please." Faro waved his hands toward the group in a request for silence. Questions continued to abound. Faro eventually cupped his hands around his mouth. "Silence, please! Now, everybody, I'm sorry about the uproar out there, I really didn't expect such a turnout."

"Turnout for what?" someone asked.

"What's the press mean by 'new management'?" another asked.

"Everyone, please," Faro repeated when the mélange of voices began to take on new life. "Now the press is aware of our family retreat because I told them. I thought we could use the occasion to handle a little PR," he said as the family began to go wild again.

"Folks, think of how positive a sign our stockholders will take this to know how hard we're working to become a united front."

"Why would they come all the way up here to watch

us hold hands and sing love songs around the fireplace?" someone queried.

"You're right." Faro smiled. "Chances are we've got so much company because they're hoping all the love and togetherness would turn foul and they'll have a story."

"After what happened yesterday, the press might get their story if they wait a little longer."

"Everybody, please," Faro urged as the nervous pitch of combined voices rose. "Maybe it'd be a good idea to take a break for a day or two, just to relax and enjoy the beauty of Tielle's place."

Tielle waited for some slight against her place of business. There was little dissent, and she gave a prayer of thanks for small favors.

"Does that sound good to everyone?"

A low murmur of voices seemed to agree with Faro's suggestion. He looked toward Tielle. "Sorry about this, Ti. Will changing things around upset the events planned for us this week?"

"We can make it work," Tielle said.

Faro nodded, turned back to his family. "Enjoy a great breakfast, folks, and we'll see each other for lunch and dinner."

"Whew, that was a lucky break," Laura noted, watching the group.

"Yeah…" Tielle sighed. "Lucky…"

Following another colder shower, Grae decided to give Leo a call. The way things had ended with Tielle had Grae turned almost inside out. Having her again felt like sheer joy. Yet that joy was marred by the realization that his excitement had thrown his aggression into such a state that he'd bruised her. He should've anticipated that. He was always a tad overly aggressive when he'd gone too long without her. Not to mention him being under added stress with the goings-on of the supposed family retreat.

He was ready to force his brother's hand, put an end to this and focus on repairing things with his ex-wife. Grae didn't know if it was just a stretch of bad timing or a sign of things not to be when Leo called and told him he was on his way up there and why.

Grae was too stunned to be angry. "What's he want with the land deed?"

"You should talk to Des about that, son," Leo said.

"Why would she go along with that—giving Faro that deed?"

"I only hold her power of attorney," Leo said. "All the rest is for her to share, but your father left that thing with her for a reason. We both know Ken intended for you to have it when Desree passes on."

"And my brother's strong-arming her for it." Grae seemed to be speaking to himself. He leaned back against the pillow-lined headboard of his bed and recalled the strange exchange he'd witnessed between his brother and aunt the day before.

"It's time to do what I'd planned before all this crap got underway. Turn around, Leo, save yourself a trip up here."

"Grae…man, think before you do this. Faro's a snake, but he is family, and he has support among a few. Moving forward with this plan may not fare well for you."

"Hell, Leo, I don't care about a future at Clegg." Grae pushed off the bed and applied a harsh massage to the back of his neck. "I've given way too much of myself to that place already, and I wound up losing what I value most."

"Look, I'm already halfway there," Leo said. "Just wait till I get there or at least until after you talk to Des."

"There's no waiting, Leo. It's already done."

"What?" Leo only needed a moment to answer his own question. "You've gone through with it but haven't told anyone?"

"Only a few needed to know." Grae drew closer to the windows overlooking a forested expanse of the property. "After Ti divorced me, I was so insane I—I put it all in motion, made plans for my revenge on Faro. I blamed him for losing Tel, when it was me and my…ways… Even so, I never said anything. Part of me still hoped there was a relationship to salvage with my brother. Stupid, huh?"

"No, man, no… So where do things stand?"

"If you're on your way here, chances are I can tell you that in person."

"Talk to Des," Leo urged.

"I will," Grae promised with a sigh. "But I think tolerating Faro has played itself out."

"Remember, he brought the family there. His plan is to bring you guys together. It'll make you look like the black hat to set things in motion that'll tear that apart."

"Has to be done." Grae turned his back on the view. "My family's been torn apart for over a year. Guess I'm a little lacking in the sympathy department for anybody else."

"Grae—"

"See you when you get here, Leo."

"Looks like the bulk of the media's losing interest." Laura sounded exhausted when she entered the office. "Chances are we'll still have a few stragglers, though."

"It's hard to call off the dogs once they smell blood." Tielle reared back in her desk chair. "We'll just have to deal with it. With any luck, this'll be over soon without the place being any worse for wear."

"I need coffee." Laura tugged on the tassels hanging from her casual tan knit sweater. The cook staff provided a cart stocked with fresh coffee and tea every day around noon. Laura was making sure her coffee held just the right amount of cream and sugar when a knock fell upon the office door.

"Mrs. Clegg," Laura greeted Desree when she saw the woman in the hall.

"Des?" Tielle stood behind her desk, a mix of delight and surprise on her face.

A soft smile curved Desree's mouth. "Can we talk for a minute?"

"Please." Tielle rounded her desk while waving toward the office living area.

"Would you like some tea, Mrs. Clegg?" Laura was already heading back to the cart.

Desree nodded, her smile remaining. "That'd be nice." She chose a spot on the sofa.

"Looks like we've got a reprieve," Tielle said once Laura had provided Desree with her tea and left the room. "It was good of Faro to suggest we break for a couple of days."

Desree absently stirred her tea. "That's what I came to talk to you about, child."

"Des?" Tielle's smile shadowed with concern. "You okay?"

"I want you to get Grae out of here."

"What? Des, uh—"

"Just take him someplace where it can be the two of you."

"Desree, why?"

"Lord, Tielle, couldn't you both use time away from all this?" Desree's teacup clattered in sync with her tense words. She set aside the cup and saucer. "Do you still love my nephew, or has the year changed things?"

Tielle bristled. "No, Des, a year hasn't changed anything. But something's wrong here, and getting Grae, of all people, to leave in the midst of it will be beyond impossible."

"Honey, please." Desree rolled her eyes as a playful light returned to her face. "It won't matter *what's* going on here. As long as he can be with you, he'll be happy as a clam. Do you really still love him, baby?"

"I really do." Tielle's confirmation held no hesitation. "Why are you pushing this, Des? It has to do with more than sending me and Grae off for private time, doesn't it? Has Faro done something?"

"Nothing I can't handle." Des retrieved her teacup.

"Then—"

"But I can only handle it if Grae *isn't* here."

"Des!" Tielle gaped. "How do you expect me to go off and leave my business with this kind of upheaval in the wind?"

"Honey, your staff is a marvel." Des sipped at the fragrant herbal blend filling her cup. "I'm sure they're fully capable of handling this family, but *I* need to handle Faro, and I can't do that with Graedon around."

Tielle smoothed shaking hands across her cotton skirt in an attempt to dry her damp palms. "He was never worth it, was he? Faro? Me standing up for him and trying to mend fences between him and Grae? I threw my marriage away for nothing, didn't I?"

"Honey." Desree set down her tea again and then scooted closer to Tielle, squeezing her hands and giving them a tug. "What happened between you and Grae was between *you* and Grae. Faro was only an issue that shed light on a bigger problem. When the two of you focus on *that* problem, that's when you'll start to mend the only fence that matters—the one between the two of you."

"What happens if we can't?" Tielle watched her fingers, entwined with Desree's, grow blurred beneath her moistening gaze. "What happens if Faro's…dealings… put us in another bad place?"

"You don't worry over that." Desree squeezed Tielle's hands again. "That's for me to handle. All I need is for you and Grae to get out of here tonight."

Tielle was more stunned than ever by then. "Des, I can't just head off for some lover's retreat just like that." She snapped her fingers.

"Tielle." Des shook her head. "Sweetie, if I know my nephew, he'll soon get tired of pretending he cares about this family stuff and press for time with you, business be damned. My guess is Grae won't offer any apologies for leaving you precious little time for anything other than him." She reached for her tea, took a healthy sip and dabbed her mouth with a napkin. Moments later, she left the office as coolly as she'd arrived.

Lunch was a surprisingly quiet affair held in the main dining room. Tielle had arranged to meet there with Laura to draft revised plans for the rest of the week.

"I'm sorry to leave you with all this on your plate so I can go traipsing off for romance."

Laura gave her colleague a knowing look. "I'm surprised you guys waited *this* long. My guess is you could've used a trip like this months ago."

"Humph, try a year." Tielle scooted her chair closer to the table then. "You call me for anything. Anytime, you hear?"

Laura lifted her brows. "Anytime?"

"Stop." Tielle rolled her eyes but couldn't help smiling. "There's a strong chance he'll refuse my offer."

Laura began to cut into her salad. "Girl, even *I* know your ex-husband better than that."

"Yeah." Tielle sighed out a laugh. "So do— I'll be damned…" Her eyes narrowed in recognition when she saw Grae passing the dining room's wide entryway with Leonard Cartright. "Let's finish this later." She tapped a finger to the table and set off to catch up with the men.

"I didn't realize you were so close when we talked before," Grae said as he and Leo walked the mural-lined corridor.

"Faro wants the deed by Friday." Leo grimaced. "Figured I'd better get out of town ASAP before business called me back to the firm."

"What's his rush?"

"Guess we'll know Friday."

Grae muttered an expletive. "I want to get this over with, Leo."

"I know, man, I know." Leo clapped Grae's shoulder. "Just don't act too hasty on whatever you have in mind, all right? I know you're at the end of your rope with Faro—"

"What's he got on you?" Grae's expression sharpened with suspicion. "I could see it before when I overheard Faro talking to Des, and I see it now on your face. What is it?"

Leo's dark face seemed to tighten with curiosity. "What'd you hear?"

"Leo?"

The men turned to see Tielle approaching them. She beamed while holding out her arms toward Leo.

"What are you doing here?"

"Came to drop off some papers." Leo enveloped Tielle in a bear hug and kissed her cheek. "Business stuff," he added.

"Sorry for interrupting." She glanced toward Grae.

Grae's focus, however, had shifted from his uncle to settle on his ex. "No need to apologize. He's not here to see me."

"Ah…" Tielle smiled toward Leo again. "Well, I hope to see you before you go." She stepped close for another hug and kiss from the man and then turned to Grae. "Can I talk to you?"

His bronze stare adopted a wolfish gleam. "Alone," he stated. It was a subtle reminder of his earlier warning that she not find herself alone with him if she didn't want to be detained.

"You two go on, Tielle." Leo gave an affectionate squeeze to her wrist and then took advantage of the opportunity to escape further questions from Grae. "We'll meet up later," he said in passing.

Grae barely noticed the man's departure. "Are we talking in my room or yours?"

She worked to ignore the suggestion in his voice. "My office."

"Hmm…" The gesture held a growling effect. "Sounds like fun."

Tielle rolled her eyes, took Grae by the arm and led him off. "Everyone seems content," she observed on their way past the dining room.

Grae wasn't impressed. "They're eating."

Tielle had to laugh.

"Are you all right?" Grae asked the instant Tielle pushed her office door shut behind him.

Tielle frowned, bewildered by the question.

Mumbling a curse, Grae advanced and squeezed her arm.

Memory surfaced when discomfort barely throbbed. "I told you I was fine," she said.

"You were lying then. I'd like the truth now."

"Grae, what exactly do you want me to say?" She slapped her hands to her sides. "What? That in a show of brute force, you misused my body in pursuit of your own selfish pleasure?"

"Tel…" Grae breathed out her name while running the tip of his thumb across his brow.

"Please believe I'm fine." She moved closer to smile up at him. "I'm better than fine. Better than I've been in a long time. You didn't do anything I didn't want or approve of."

"Don't lie to me." The order was gruff.

She smiled pityingly. "I never have and I'm not about to start now. Good enough?"

"It'll do." He used the closeness she'd risked to his advantage and drew her high against him.

"This isn't why I called you here."

"I know." He was already taking her into the office living area.

"Grae, come on, listen to me." She slapped his shoulder. "I need to ask you something."

"Mmm-hmm." He doused her neck with the most luxurious glides from his mouth. All the while he unraveled the wrap tie of her shirt. "It's okay, I have condoms."

"Idiot." She punched his shoulder that time. "This isn't about that."

Grae lifted his head. "It's not?"

"Not exactly."

"Right." He went back to nibbling her ear.

The act sent Tielle falling under the spell of his touch. She summoned additional strength to her voice. "Be serious."

Eventually, Grae obeyed her orders. His expression was unreadable as he studied her, waiting for her to say what she would.

"Come away with me."

He blinked. Her words were clearly not what he expected. "Come away with you and do what?" he asked.

She bit her lip and glanced toward the sofa he held her over. "Whatever you want. Talk."

"And?"

Tielle sent a silent curse toward Des. Not that she minded going away with her ex, but there was a storm brewing. It was definitely not the time for her to be away.

She rolled her eyes back toward his very nice face. "Whatever you want, Grae," she assured him and felt her heart leap when his extraordinary eyes narrowed and raked her body lying prone beneath his.

"Whatever I want. Anything."

The question-non-question statements adequately dampened her panties. "Wouldn't be much fun otherwise." Her response was steady.

"Sounds damn good. When do we leave?" His voice was a rumble when he resumed his nibbling on her ear, freeing her from the shirt once he'd laid her down.

Tielle was fast approaching the point of speechlessness. Grae was manipulating a nipple between his thumb and forefinger while his free hand occupied space beneath the rising hem of her skirt. His fingers teased the lacy stitching of her lingerie.

"You'd really leave with all that's going on?" His voice was maddeningly calm, as though he were doing nothing out of the ordinary.

"I think that's why." Her voice was a rush of breath. "This is more than I expected when I—I agreed to it."

"Sorry I made you get involved." He took in the emotions crossing her face as he touched her.

"I—" her lashes wouldn't still "—I couldn't say no."

He brought his forehead to hers. "I don't always leave you much room to do that, do I?"

"I can hold my own…mmm… Y-you shouldn't think so highly of your abilities…"

His grin was devilment displayed. "My abilities are nothin' to underestimate." He returned to lay siege to her earlobe, assaulting it with his lips, teeth and tongue, and continued the affecting caresses along her panties' stitching.

Chapter 11

Tielle's office was colored by the rich sounds of delight being granted. Faintly, she chastised herself for being insatiable. After all, she'd had the pleasure of Graedon Clegg just that morning, the night before...

Another self-chastisement intervened just then. She was reminding herself of how long she'd been without him. While a year was perhaps not such a lengthy duration of abstinence, it was far lengthier than what she was used to, given who her lover was.

Grae's sexual appetite was as big as he was—if not bigger. If Tielle had somehow forgotten that, she recollected it all within the first ten minutes.

Grae had tired of skirting his fingers along the edge of her panties. He insinuated two inside the crotch. The sensation of flesh to flesh had Tielle biting down so hard on her lip, she threatened to draw blood. She strained beneath him, seeking to improve her position in order to receive every aspect of his caress.

"Mmm... Not now, Grae... No time for this..." Her mouth and body had taken differing trains of thought.

Grae had unwrapped Tielle's shirt, unbuttoned her khaki skirt like she was his own pleasure provider. He undid the front clasp of her bra and swirled his tongue on a budding nipple while his fingers eased deeper inside her. His mouth curved beneath the satisfaction roused by her breathy cries near his ear. The suckling he applied to the firm tip of her breast was as desire maddened as his intimate exploration of her body.

"Grae, I can't—can't come out of my clothes... Grae..."

"Too late," he growled between the valley of dark chocolate.

Tielle discovered that her clothing had served as a mere pallet for her body against the sofa. The sofa left only a scant bit of space for his big frame to maneuver in. Tielle didn't know whether she wanted to celebrate or be disappointed by that fact.

Grae was obviously disappointed, for he cursed viciously when the sofa refused to accommodate his plans for her body. "I'm taking you to a bed."

"Grae, wait." She gave his forearms a squeeze when he would've gathered her up from the sofa. "Just give me a few hours to get some things squared away and then I'm all yours."

Her word choice seemed to cool his ardor. "You haven't been *all mine* in over a year."

"We can discuss it while we're away." She sought to cool the temper she saw stirring in his eyes.

"How long?"

"Just a few hours. Two at the most," she tacked on with haste when his gaze narrowed. She figured her fate was sealed when her attempts to slow her breathing only sent his eyes faltering to her chest.

"Grae..." Her sigh wavered when he dipped his head to begin another possessive examination of her nipples.

Beneath gentle nudges from his nose, he shared his attention between her taut and glistening pebbles.

He let only the tip of his tongue touch her body. Faintly, he encircled her areolas, ignoring the nipples that bumped his mouth each time she inhaled. Her panties were uncomfortably damp—a side effect of his attentions, but one she was unable to do anything about.

Needy, Tielle rubbed the sensational ridge of denim-clad muscle that was pronounced and hard where it pressed against her belly.

"All right then." He favored a nipple with one last skillful tug and then set her bra to rights. "Handle your business." He wrapped her back into her shirt and buttoned her skirt. "I'll meet you out back?" Expectancy pooled in his entrancing stare as he waited for her to confirm or correct. At her nod, he relieved her of his weight and drew her up to sit on the sofa.

"Pack light." He cupped her face. "Don't make me come looking for you." He kissed her mouth, granted her a wink and was gone from the office without further hesitation.

Tielle waited until she heard the door lock click and then quickly tended her clothes and hair while scooting to the edge of the sofa. She pushed herself half off, reconsidered and reclaimed her prone position in an effort to make sense of her ex's sudden and unsettling return to her life. She failed miserably at the task, a fact that didn't surprise her in the least.

"It's probably not a good idea for you to stay for this."

"Forget it." Leo slanted a look down the conference room table to Desree. "Especially when you just told me that you asked Ti to get Grae out of here."

Desree rolled her eyes. "I can handle Faro."

"Can you? Giving him that deed is lunacy."

"It's the only way to quiet him down."

"That's a crock. Faro's never been trustworthy." Leo tugged at his shirt cuffs and snorted. "You're a fool, Des, if you think he only wants that deed as a memento of his father."

"It's a chance I'll have to take."

"And if it blows up in your face?"

Desree slammed her hand against the table. "Dammit, Leo, what more can I do?"

"Talk to Grae."

"And you call *me* a fool?" Desree practically sneered. "Why would you suggest that?"

Leo shrugged. "Should've been done long ago."

"The child's just blowing a lot of hot air." Desree fidgeted with the stylishly frayed sleeves of her sweater. "Once he has this—" she reached for the folder containing the land deed to the Clegg Marketing Park "—it'll be over."

"Des…" Leo closed his eyes.

"*You* know how much he thinks of Tielle. For him to do what you're thinking would hurt her as much as Grae." She shook her head. "Maybe there's a part of him that won't risk that."

"Desree, no one means as much to Faro as Faro." Leo swiveled the chair he occupied at the head of the table. "The only reason he settled down when Tielle was in the picture was because he probably thought she could get Grae to step down and let him have the top spot. I believe he thought her attachment to this place—" he extended his hands toward the ceiling "—would have her wanting to come back here and take Grae with her.

"Grae let his drama with Faro blind him to the fact that he was losing his wife. How do you think Ti will react knowing she'd stood up for someone willing to hurt the man she loves this way?"

Desree rested her head in her hands. "You want *me* to be the one to talk to Grae, but I can't put that in his head."

"And if Faro puts it there?" Leo challenged.

Desree sighed. "I just want them all out of here. If giving him this deed has a chance in hell of accomplishing that, then I have to see it through."

A smile cracked his face then. "You're one stubborn woman. All right, then. I've got no desire to witness what I know is coming, but I'll be damned if I leave you here to handle it on your own."

Leo's voice fell silent just as a knock landed on the conference room door.

"Come in," Desree called. Her lips thinned as Faro walked inside.

"Got your message, Aunty," he said. His angular, dark face appeared guarded when he noticed Leo in the room. He greeted the man with a stiff nod then looked to Des with mock expectancy. "Well?" he prompted.

"Right here." Tielle pointed toward a paved, tree-lined road while giving Grae directions.

"I remember, Tel." His voice was quiet. He'd insisted on driving and had barely spoken a word since they'd left the retreat.

Tielle regarded him closer then. Even in profile, he looked rather subdued, and she figured their locale had much to do with that.

They had spent their wedding night at Brunch and Memories. The secluded bed-and-breakfast wasn't far from Turner Estates and Gardens. The two businesses shared such an easy coexistence, in fact, that all couples who exchanged vows at Turner Estates received a complimentary wedding-night stay at Brunch and Memories as part of their wedding package.

Tielle remembered that she and Grae had so enjoyed the perk that they extended their stay to include two additional nights before jetting off to begin their honeymoon. She felt herself growing a bit more subdued when the B and B came into view.

"I miss you, Tel," Grae said once he'd parked the SUV and sat looking out at the inviting brick-and-stone structure beyond the windshield.

"I never wanted to go," she said.

"I was a bullheaded idiot."

"Yes," Tielle confirmed, smiling when she heard his chuckle.

"There're things you need to hear me say, Tel. Things you deserve to hear."

"I'm ready to listen." She studied her hands clasped in her lap. "I was always ready to hear it. I was an idiot, too. I should've never walked away before I made you tell me everything you wouldn't—everything I knew you needed to."

Grae took her hand from her lap. He toyed with her fingers before he kissed them. "That'll be difficult here," he said.

It was true. They'd made love all over the place and *in* places that they were surely not allowed to. All Grae wanted was to revisit those places, to improve on those vivid memories if that were at all possible.

"I'm gonna have to count on you to be the cooler head," he told her.

She laughed. "What good will that do against you and your plans to improve our memories of this place?"

Her tease didn't have the intended effect, and Grae's expression was a stony one. "I know I bullied you throughout a lot of our marriage. The fact that you were always so hell-bent on pleasing me was why I thought you were lying to me about not hurting you the other night."

She gave a slight wince. "My grandmothers always said, 'If you treat your husband like a king, he'll treat you like a queen.'"

Grae smirked. "Your grannies were lucky to find men deserving of the crown. Thinking like that has gotten a lot of women in trouble. I think it got you in more than your fair share with me."

"Grae—"

"Just let me say this, Tel, please." He squeezed her hand, keeping it trapped on a denim-clad thigh. "I pressed my advantage. A lot. Wore you down when you leaned toward doing things I wasn't in favor of."

She turned on the suede seating to face him fully. "I never had brothers or sisters. I thought you needed to get along with yours."

"Tel, I'm not talking about Faro. I'm talking about you wanting to come back here to Vancouver long before we divorced. You wanted to run the place for your family. Do you remember what I did when you told me that?"

She tried to tug her hand free of his. Grae wouldn't let her. She raised a narrowed gaze to his face. "You didn't bully me."

"I kept you in bed two days. *Convincing* you how much I needed you to be there for me."

"It wasn't unreasonable for you to want that." She

smiled sadly. "Vancouver isn't a place I'd want to com-mute to and from Portland every day. Not the best move for a married couple who like each other." She put her hand over his. "And I can think of a lot more unpleasant ways to be bullied."

"Then let's talk about how I bullied you with Faro."

"Let's not. I can think of so many other things I'd prefer to do."

"Such as?"

"Such as…" She settled her head to the rest and sighed. "Improving our memories. I think you said some-thing about having whatever you wanted. *Anything* you wanted…"

"I remember."

"And?"

The word had barely passed her lips when Grae reached for her, tugging her unceremoniously across the gear changer. They launched a kiss that deepened quickly, tumbling into a realm that was equal parts lust and desperation. Tielle was practically straddling his lap seconds into the X-rated kiss that had her chanting his name without shame.

"We need to get out of this car…"

Tielle smiled through the throaty kiss. "Finally… something we agree on…"

"What'd you do?" Tielle blurted upon realizing the bellman was bypassing the short stairway to the inn's suites.

"Anything I want, remember?"

"Within reason," she grated.

Grae gave her a sidelong glance. "Where's the fun in that?"

"Will you at least tell me where we're going?" she whispered.

"We're going to improve on a memory," he whispered back.

Immediately, Tielle began to file through the numerous and naughty acts she and her new husband had indulged in at Brunch and Memories so long ago. It seemed like another lifetime.

Her cheeks burned at the possibilities. "They won't allow that."

"Are you serious?" Grae's voice was hushed and amused. "You supply almost half their business."

She had to laugh despite the bellman's close proximity. "Don't use me to advance your perverted interests."

"Interests I only endeavor in with one woman."

"How'd I get so lucky?" She sighed, sobering when their escort took them down a long, silent corridor.

Tielle felt her breath hitch when she saw they were headed toward the pair of imposing red oak doors at the end of the hallway. The maple placard, engraved in gold lettering above the doors, read Billiards.

"Grae." Her fingers tightened reflexively on his arm.

Grae merely kept moving along behind the bellman. Tielle managed to keep up with his long strides, though she was more focused on swallowing the sizable ball lodged in her throat.

Somehow, the ball increased its size when Tielle preceded Grae and the bellman into the billiards room. An enormous pool table was adorned with plump king-size pillows and fern-green fleece blankets. Heavy russet-brown drapes were closed to permit bronze wall sconces to drench the atmosphere in a soothing golden glow.

"The luggage is in the garden suite, sir." The bellman gave away nothing that would hint of any curiosity he may've had over what was about to take place in the room. He handed Grae an old-fashioned brass key and shook hands when Grae thanked him with a fifty-dollar tip.

"Please call if you need anything further." The bellman sent a polite nod and smile in Tielle's direction. He sent another look toward Grae. "Enjoy your stay, sir."

"Grae," Tielle said once the bellman left.

There was no opportunity for further discussion. Grae hoisted her high against his solid chest.

"I've been meaning to thank you for choosing the dresses you've been wearing." His fingers skimmed the tie of the wrap dress she wore with low-cut black leather boots. "So easy to get you out of," he murmured while bathing her earlobe with his tongue.

Tielle allowed herself to melt, knowing she was on her way to becoming a complete puddle in a matter of seconds. Grae manipulated the ultrasensitive fleshly lobe of her ear with several dry tugs from his beautifully sculpted mouth. Again, he brought his tongue into the act, infrequently soothing the shell of her ear before delving inside and then exploring the satiny outer patch of skin surrounding it.

Her hands rested, half curved, at his shoulders and shook faintly. Tielle clenched them into fists when she felt him untying her dress.

"Grae…" Her tone urged caution, but she knew it would do no good. Determination defined his gorgeous honey-toned face as he focused on every part of her he bared to his brilliant eyes.

One flick of his fingers released the barrette she'd used to secure her thick hair into a more manageable ponytail. Tielle pounded once against the wall of granite that was his chest.

"We can't," she said.

Grae laid her down and removed her bra with an experienced touch.

"We'll ruin the table," she worried when his fingers skimmed her panties.

During their previous visit to Brunch and Memories, the couple had only indulged in a bit of light foreplay. They'd remained fully clothed until the need for a more private venue sent them upstairs. Now, Grae had tugged Tielle's panties so that the garment barely clung to her lush upper thighs. Cradling her bare bottom, he positioned her to his satisfaction.

"Grae—"

"Shh… Don't worry about it. I bought the table."

"How'd you plan this?" Her lovely dark face was a picture of awe and anticipation.

Grae surveyed her steadily, possession blatant in his fantastic stare. "While you handled your business, I've handled some of my own."

"You—" A moaning cry took the place of her question. His mouth skimmed her toned belly, the tip of his tongue outlining her navel.

Grae curved his palms about her thighs, drawing her down to the edge of the sturdy pine table.

Any concerns about the structure became irrelevant for Tielle. Her only interest was on the pleasure blooming throughout her body. Decadence accompanied pleasure, and she indulged in its drugging capabilities. Grae soon had her practically naked and splayed out like a seductive offering upon the table. He'd insinuated his rigid frame between her legs and proceeded to take his pleasure most enthusiastically.

Her responding cries were throaty, echoing when he touched her again. Tielle felt his breath feather over her skin when he shushed her. The action only succeeded in riddling her with a wave of shudders, and her exposed sex puckered more persistently for the kiss it anticipated.

Grae's first intention was to torture Tielle with the faint brushes his mouth cascaded across the bare patch of skin above her femininity. Next, his nose trailed a naughty outline around her clit, the tip nudging insistently about the stimulated bundle of nerves when she arched into his touch.

She tried to open herself more to him—difficult with the undergarments still holding her thighs captive in addition to his hands secured about her fleshy limbs. Were it not for his overtly possessive hold, Tielle would've jackknifed right off the table. Grae replaced his nose with the tip of his talented tongue and retraced a sensual circle about the part of her anatomy he tended to.

Tielle writhed about in frustration, wanting very much to be free of her panties—the only scrap of clothing still adorning her body. The silky whiskers of a close-cut beard consistently raked the powder-soft flesh of her inner thighs. The sensation it roused encouraged Tielle's hands to begin a seductive trek toward her upper body.

She smoothed her palms up her torso and about the twin circumferences of her breasts, along the elegant line of her neck, and then she burrowed them in her thick, captivating mane. All the while she arched, squirmed and trembled beneath Grae's attention.

For a moment, he left her bereft of his touch. Then, caging her body under his, he pleasured her with his thumb rotating against the bundle of sensitivity above her intimate folds. Satisfaction offered a different kind of heat as he delighted in watching her caress the dark cocoa expanse of her curvy body. A smile narrowed his gaze when he saw her mouth form an *O*.

She'd be flooding his hand with her moisture soon, he predicted.

He slowed the rotation against the tight bud of nerves set to usher in climax. Tielle caught his wrist, preventing any plans he had for escape. Grae lowered himself nearer to her, tormenting her with a slow, wet suck to her nipples.

"Trust me," he urged, patting her hip.

She whimpered, the sound tapering into a startled grunt when she felt her panties being jerked free of her body. Graedon closed the delicate garment into a thick fist and pushed it into a back jean pocket. His mouth blazed a trail down her torso, teeth barely grazing her skin as he journeyed to the part of her he throbbed for.

Grae spread her to his satisfaction, but didn't claim her right away. Instead, he glided his way around what she insistently arched toward him. Tielle bumped her fists against the velvety green surface of the pool table. She was close to out of her mind with want. Her toes flexed and then attempted to grasp at his denims where her feet bumped his powerful thighs. Blindly, she reached for him, hoping to press his head to her preferred spot.

Grae didn't make her wait long, and they both filled the room with appreciative groans when his tongue filled her. Tielle bent into an elegant bow, taking more of his driving tongue.

Grae wanted to devour her, the moisture and fragrance of her core driving him insane with hunger and the need to dominate. Her hips bucked more the deeper he invaded, until he stilled her with one hand pressuring her stomach.

The soft gesture encouraged her to follow his direction. "Mmm-mmm."

Impatient to bathe more of her core, his hands flexed on her thighs. He took her hips off the table, bringing her higher while allowing him to stand at almost his full height.

Tielle was happily at the mercy of the giant who held her, loved her and took her over a cliff of splendid desire. The feverish bucking of her hips resumed until he tightened his hold to command her to still.

He didn't shush her when she screamed at the vivid sucking he gave her silken folds, though he did grin at the whimper she gave when he brought an end to the act. Before she could add words to show her disappointment, he took her with his tongue, vigorously plundering her at length.

In a show of stunning finesse, Grae supported her with one hand while the other freed his belt and jean fastening. The denim cascaded downward toward his stylishly rugged hiking boots while he kept Tielle positioned and doffed the dark corduroy shirt he wore.

She paid no attention to his disrobing. Her mind only registered the sensation of his shadowed jaw scraping the delicate flesh of her thighs near his shoulders while her calves dangled across them. She was so driven by arousal and the intense sensation of abandon wafting through her that she took little notice of him setting their protection in place.

His sex penetrating hers was as unexpected as it was spectacular. Grae had settled her back down to the gargantuan table. His wide body kept her thighs spread to his approval, allowing him to fold his hands over the polished siding of the table and steady his stance before her.

Tielle wanted to keep her eyes open to indulge in the sight of his phenomenal chest. Unfortunately, it was impossible to keep her eyes open against the strong, repeated drives of his lean hips deepening the path for his thick erection. The perfect sensations stirred when they became too drugging, heavily weighing on her lids as she welcomed him.

Every clench of her inner muscles forced a guttural grunt up his throat, enticing him to let go and spew his need. Grae wasn't ready for the moment to end. He had imagined this particular fantasy for too long. His imagination had nothing on the reality of her pliant and willing in his hands. His legs promised a swift withdrawal of strength then. Tielle's high-pitched breaths, her lovely face, her body and the magnificent dark cloud of her hair completed the stunning picture of the fantasy he never daydreamed of becoming reality.

Chapter 12

The forecasted snow made another appearance. A light dusting at first, and then the snowfall became heavier as the morning churned on. Graedon and Tielle didn't mind in the least. Their pool table romp had been a lengthy, sexually charged event.

Tielle was sure she'd been left with a new collection of bruises and burns. None of which Grae could take credit for. All were courtesy of the table's lovely, velvety fabric. The material had been unforgiving against her bottom. Tielle figured it was a show of disapproval for how shamefully it had been used.

They made their way from the billiard room in the wee hours of the following morning. Dawn found them embraced in a spooning hold and snuggled beneath flowing bed coverings as they watched the snowfall from the suite's picture window.

"How'd you know we'd come here?" Tielle asked.

"I didn't."

She smiled, sex content, drowsy and secure in the potency of his embrace. "You'd have been out of a pretty penny with your pool table purchase if you hadn't."

"Well…" He burrowed in closer to her. "I had planned

to revert to old habits and…press the issue until you agreed to make the inn one of our stops."

Tielle laughed. Grae joined in, but the desire didn't hold long for him.

"I lied when I told you I was sorry for overreacting when I thought you'd slept with someone else," he said.

"I see."

"I don't think you do," Grae countered. "When it comes to you, I'm possessive, overbearing and chauvinistic as hell. I could probably work on the overbearing and chauvinistic parts, but I don't see myself doing anything about the possessive part. I don't see myself *wanting* to do anything about the possessive part."

"I know that, Grae."

He frowned. "You do?"

"What you're saying is nothing new." Her eyes followed the journey of a snowflake sliding down the window. "You've always been this way. Didn't take me long to realize that shortly after I met you."

Grae turned Tielle to her back, needing to look into the baby-doll allure of her face. "And you married me anyway?"

"Yes."

"Why, dammit?"

Tielle gave him a look that nearly screamed *idiot*. "I married you because I love you, and all the rest makes you who you are."

He continued to frown. "Even all that alpha male crap?"

She laughed. "Sometimes it's *especially* all that alpha male crap, and please—" she cringed "—don't make me explain all that."

Grae nodded. "I want you back, Tel. I know we have a

lot of trust to rebuild. It's gonna take time, and it's time I want to spend here."

Smiling anew, Tielle surveyed their cozy surroundings from the bed they'd been snuggled in for hours. "Sounds spectacular, but the people we work for would never allow it."

"My people won't have a choice." His features tensed. "I plan on resigning my position after this nightmare with Faro is over."

Incredulous, she pushed up to brace her weight on her elbows. "Grae, why would you do that?"

It was Grae's turn to observe his ex as if she'd lost her mind. "Have you forgotten how much of myself I've given to that place?"

"But you wanted to please your dad…"

"Right." He grimaced. "And doing that drew a line between me and my brother. Now it's just the two of us and he hates me for it." He saw the strange look she gave him and studied her with heightened curiosity. "What?"

"You just… You always talk about Faro hating you instead of you hating each other." Tielle watched him roll a massive shoulder in a lazy semblance of a shrug.

"I don't hate him," Grae uttered simply. "He's my brother. I wanted to kill him for coming between us, but I know he wasn't to blame, and like I said, he's my brother."

Tielle sat up fully, trailed her fingers across his whiskered jaw. "And you wonder why I married you."

Grae tugged her into a lazy kiss while seating her in his lap and squeezing her bottom through the sheet. He broke the kiss to speak the words into her shoulder. "You know we have to go back."

She nodded. "I knew that before we left, but Des wanted me to get you out of there."

"Ah…" Grae smiled and gave a playful frown. "So all this was pity sex?"

She linked her arms about his neck and toyed in the dark curls covering his head. "Do you feel offended?" she asked.

"Quite," he lied.

She smiled, grinding on his lap. "I can tell. Do you think we can spare some time before heading back to our responsibilities?"

"Hmm…" Grae rested back into the pillows, the move providing Tielle with a nudge from the head of his erection. A knowing smile brought a curve to the heavenly sculpting of his mouth when he noticed her lashes flutter. He was sensitive enough to pick up the slight change in her breathing.

"We should definitely take our time." He jerked her into another kiss. Turning the tables with ease, he put her on her back in the center of the magnificent bed they'd thoroughly used.

"Why aren't you still gone?!"

"Shh!" Tielle made a slicing gesture across her neck and went to close the bedroom door behind Laura. "We don't want the whole house to know we're here yet."

"'We'?" Laura glanced around the third floor of the suite. "Grae?"

"In the cabana house for now." Tielle smiled at Laura's bewildered expression. "He thought it'd be better if he kept a low profile till tonight."

"Why?"

"We both have a bad feeling about what's in store."

Tielle twisted a tank top between her hands. "There's been a lot of negativity during an event that was meant to be positive, you know?"

"So what's the plan?"

"Not sure there is one. We only want to be here in case Faro…"

"And how do you feel about that?" Laura softened her voice. "You fought so hard to convince Grae to give Faro a fair shake."

Tielle tossed the tank top back into the bag she'd been unpacking. "I'm trying not to even think about it, Laura. Maybe we're just overreacting anyway and Faro's next… surprise…will be to treat the family to a cruise around the world."

"And if it's not?"

Groaning, Tielle pushed her fingers through her hair. "Then this will be another in a long series of crazy stunts I once tried to convince my husband were all part of his own resistance to giving his brother a chance."

"Honey, please don't take on blame for another thing gone wrong." Laura pulled Tielle with her to the sofa in the room's living area.

Tielle smirked. "Doing no such thing. I just have a crazy knack for making it sound that way." She winked, and moments later joined Laura in a round of much-needed laughter.

Snowfall had been a steady and beautiful companion throughout the day. It had tapered off just after nightfall, leaving its vibrant white presence resting thickly upon the grounds, trees and brush. There had been no set plans for family gatherings since Faro's eagerly supported suggestion that the group take a break from "togetherness" to enjoy all the relaxing aids Tielle's establishment had to offer.

The suggestion did everyone more good than harm, thankfully. Tielle was even starting to put her hope in a peaceful end to the week and the beginning of repairing the damage between her and Grae. The scheduled break time for relaxation clearly didn't appear to relate to dining.

The family continued to converge upon the elegant room designated for the scrumptious meals created by the Turner cook staff. Tielle's perceptions regarding the strength of the family mood seemed solid, especially when she risked dropping in for breakfast. There, she received more than the usual amount of morning greetings. She'd even been invited to dine with a group of Grae's aunts, women not known for their overwhelming warmth.

Tielle had accepted the offer to join the women at their table and told them she'd return after a quick check-in with that morning's serving staff. The group had set up shop in the prep room just down a corridor secluded from the main dining area. She was halfway to the door when it opened and Grae stepped out.

"Going stir-crazy out in the cabana house, huh?" she asked.

Grae snared her waist and set her neatly between himself and the wall. "Going stir-crazy without you," he said while nibbling her earlobe.

"Grae…" Her eyes were already rolling back in her head. "Honey, we can't do this here." She bit her lip on the moan stirred by his tongue adding dampness to her lobe.

"I—it's not time for your family to know we—" A

groan enveloped the rest of what she had to say when his thumb sought the nipple already beaded against her shirt. He was working the nub beneath lazy circles from his thumb.

"Grae—" Her next attempt to encourage restraint was silenced by his mouth crushing hers. Lithely, his tongue engaged hers in delicious play. Her moaning adopted a less tormented tone in favor of a more delighted one.

Desree's voice interrupted them a moment later. Tielle gasped, breaking the kiss like a teenager caught doing something frowned upon. She was left no other choice than to remain between her ex and the wall.

"Hey, Des." Grae suffered no bouts of disgrace when he greeted his aunt warmly. He kept a devilish stare fixed on Tielle then turned a more guileless, adorable one toward Desree.

"Why are you back so soon?" the woman asked Tielle.

"Calm down, Des," Grae urged. "I know you asked Tel to get me out of here, but you knew I'd have to come back, especially if I thought Faro was up to something." He looked to Tielle, and his gaze raked her body twice over. "No matter how nice the enticement was to stay."

Tielle thought it best to focus on Desree and not Grae. Unfortunately, Des's gaze did even less to put her at ease. "What's going on?" Tielle asked, moving closer to the woman.

"I wished you two had listened." Hands clasped, Des gave them a shake and observed the young couple with a disappointed glare. "You could use time away more than staying here to be irritated by whatever's about to happen."

Grae moved closer to his aunt. "What do you mean, Aunt Des?"

"Could I have everybody's attention, please?"

Des began to wring her clasped hands and turned toward Faro's voice blanketing the dining room.

Grae, Tielle and Desree moved into the room to find Faro near the front. Flanking him were two men, not Cleggs, and until then not present at the retreat.

Faro noticed his brother, and the glee claiming his face took on a new sheen. "There he is now! Come in, Grae. Get comfortable."

Grae, Tielle and Des remained where they were.

"What's going on, Faro?" Oscar Clegg asked.

"Can't it wait?" another asked. "I sure don't want my breakfast ruined."

"I apologize for the timing, folks." Faro's grin negated the sincerity of the apology. "I think it's best to get this handled early in the day. I've got the feeling there will be a lot to say afterward. Best not to have those conversations lingering on into the dead of night."

"Get all of *what* handled?" Paul Clegg asked.

Faro took a theatrical breath. "I hoped this wouldn't have to happen. That folks would do the right thing—"

"Faro, don't do this." Desree moved to give the plea.

"Do what, Aunt Des? Go after my birthright?"

"Aw, man, what the hell are you talkin' about?" Gerald Clegg groaned.

"All of you know I deserve more than what I've been given! I busted my ass for Dad all my life, and in the end what'd it get me? Baby brother being positioned as *my* boss?"

A collective groan filled the room. Many had heard Faro's complaint before and often.

"Are you ever gonna let this go?" Asia asked her

cousin. "Uncle Ken obviously had his reasons for leaving Grae in charge."

"And thank God he did," Barry Clegg called out. "Our pockets haven't hurt a day since Grae took the chair."

"How fortunate," Faro sneered. "Still doesn't make it right. Grae's successes shouldn't mean that I have to be denied what should've been mine in the first place."

"Don't matter now anyway," someone said. "Ken's dead and his will says that he wanted Grae to take his place."

"My father's will said a lot of things, and it just so happens I hold the deed to the land where Clegg Marketing Park stands."

"So?"

Faro smiled at the question. "Kenneth Clegg's will clearly states that any family member in possession of this deed could claim the position as CEO if the deed holder feels the company's current leadership is unworthy."

The family members began to shift ever more restlessly in their seats as though they were coming to realize what Faro was threatening.

"This is goin' too far, Faro," someone said.

"Yeah, man, it's time to end these issues with Grae. He's your baby brother."

A few in the room looked to Grae. Clearly, they expected him to challenge Faro. Grae remained silent, his cool, bronze gaze betraying nothing.

"I'm well within my right to see this through." Faro smirked. "In time, you guys will see that."

"Why'd you bring us up here for this, Faro?" Barry asked. "Do you really think any of us would support you carrying out such a disgrace?"

"You should think about that word, Uncle Barry. *Disgrace.* I think there're many disgraces that've been carried out over the years."

"Faro, that's enough!" Desree spat. "Think before you do this."

"Why, Des? My father didn't think before he put a—" Faro bowed his head then and sighed. "Dad didn't think once before he put someone with no experience, no clue of how the game is played, in charge of the business when he was gone. Grae played around in school while I worked my ass off in class and internships to graduate with honors. I have damn well earned my chance to sit at the helm, and the strength of my grades is least among the reasons why.

"I waited." Faro shook his head. "Waited to go after what was mine, hoping I could be the kind of upstanding man some believed me to be." He looked at Tielle. "It was just too much to stand by and be passed over at every turn in favor of a disgrace."

"Faro, you—"

"I may not have had your grades or your experience," Grae's voice resounded over that of a male cousin who stood to champion him, "but I do have a passable idea of how the game is played, Faro. I'm not the only one who took a close look at Dad's will. It states that any family member in possession of the deed and employed by the firm has the power to make a challenge for the authority seat."

Faro nodded, his grim smile reflecting the hint of satisfaction. "Glad you understand the strength of the claim."

"I do, but I wonder if you do." Grae sent a nod toward the portfolio he'd waved about like a banner. "It's gonna take more than that deed. You're gonna need a position at the firm, which I'm afraid you no longer have."

"Oh, Grae." Faro chuckled. "I'm afraid it's a little too late to try and boot me from the company now."

"I'm not booting you from the company *now,* Faro. I booted you from the company four months ago."

A hush fell upon the room. All the murmured conversations silenced. The audience looked from Grae to Faro. It was as though they were observing a vicious tennis match and were in anticipation of the next ferocious serve.

"Nice try." Faro's grin lost a bit of its brightness.

From his jacket pocket, Grae produced an envelope. "You've been out since June," he said. "You're there now pretty much in name only. I didn't want to announce it to make it formal. I kept hoping I'd see a shred of that upstanding man I've been told you have the potential to be."

Grae began to make his way from the back of the dining room. "Instead, I saw the petty, scheming, backstabbing one I've known all my life. Like you, I battled with bringing more drama into the family." He slanted Faro a wink, letting the man glimpse his insincerity. "And just when I decided to announce that you no longer had a place at Clegg, I hear about this retreat to heal the family.

"Every part of me knew that you were spouting a bunch of bull, but like a fool I hoped…and then there were other reasons I thought the trip was worth my time." Grae looked to Tielle, who sat at a table with her head bowed. He turned back to his brother.

"But that's what you were counting on, wasn't it? For Tel to keep me distracted? Good strategy, when hearing her name is enough to take my mind off everything." He nodded. "Good strategy."

"This is trite." Faro waved his hand dismissively. "Lies—trying to overshadow the truth. You're out, Grae."

Grae was passing the envelope to a man seated at a table to his left. "The board met to hold a vote following my request that they discuss your removal. Seems more than a few of them had grown sick of your antics over the years. They knew it'd take a family member to set motions in place to get you out."

"And *you're* that family member?"

Desree moved closer. "Faro—"

"Uncle Barry, are those the documents you and the other board members drew up and signed?"

Barry nodded. "They are." He passed the papers to his brothers at the table.

"I thought it'd be a good idea to not be the only Clegg the board heard from involving this. Barry, Paul and Gerald were very much in favor of having you removed. Pass that copy to him," Grae instructed Paul, who now held the document. "It's his to keep."

"If you check your e-mail, you'll find a copy's been sent to you electronically. Enjoy your land," Grae said. "There's plenty of it despite the acreage Clegg takes up. I'm sure someone as crafty as you can think up a good use for it. So long as you stay out of my way, we'll be able to coexist just fine."

The paperwork had finally made its way to the front of the room where Faro stood reviewing it stoically. Grae watched his brother for a while and then nodded and headed from the silent room. Gradually, the remaining guests exited, as well. Tielle observed the devastation throwing Faro's dark face into shadow. She refused to let herself feel sympathy and discovered she had finally been drained of it all.

Chapter 13

"Don't ask me to apologize for that, Tel."

Grae had gone out to the enclosed terrace just off from the lower-level sitting room when he left the breakfast. He'd known his refuge wouldn't last long, and had hoped Tielle would be the first—and only—one to find him. Within minutes of her arrival, however, he discovered that her being there wasn't providing the calm he'd come to expect when she was near.

Despite the terrace's electronically activated glass enclosures, the area carried a noticeable chill. Tielle rubbed her arms, hoping to stimulate warmth beneath the fabric of her blouse sleeves.

"I wasn't planning on asking you that." She shortened the distance between them.

"Why's that?" Slowly, he turned to study her from his perch on the back of one of the terrace sofas.

Her lips thinned. "Maybe he deserved it."

Tielle's words didn't go as far with Grae as they might have. His extraordinary gaze thinned to reflect irritation. "Maybe he'd *always* deserved it."

"Grae, I didn't come to argue—"

"'Course not, since that would mean admitting you were wrong about my jackass of a brother all the times

I tried to tell you he wasn't worth a shred of your damn time."

"Grae?" Tielle regarded him incredulously. "You couldn't have known that then. You had no basis—"

"Basis, Tel?" he roared, bolting from the sofa. "Try every day of hell he put me through while we grew up under the same roof! I think that'd give me a *little* context for my opinion, don't you?"

Cringing, Tielle knew she couldn't argue his point. She didn't want to. "You're right."

"About damn time." Grae smirked, resistant to any peacemaking attempts. "All it took was four years of drama involving that fool and a divorce that's kept us separated for a year."

Tielle felt her slow-to-rise temper begin a definite simmer. Her cognac-colored stare flashed with brilliant fury. "Don't *you* forget that *you* were the one who set our divorce in motion."

"What was that?" His voice went dangerously low. He invaded her space, pretending not to have heard her.

"Is that why you came to see me that day?" she asked, refusing to be cowed. "You wanted me to agree to Faro having the retreat here, knowing all along that you planned to use this place to hash this all out."

"Faro already had plans to bring you in on it. I only wanted to ensure you went for it."

Disgust fueled the snort she gave. "In spite of everything we've gone through about him, you throw me back in this hell."

His smile held no humor. "You'd have been in it regardless. Faro would've run down some line to get you on board with his plan. Given his track record with drawing you over to his side…I only came to see you because this all gave me an excuse to do so, and when it's all said and done, I'd have tried anything to get him out of the business.

"It was only a matter of time before all the questionable crap Faro pulled over there screwed the family anyway." He shrugged, spreading his hands. "Guess you were right, Tel, and I'm the bad guy in this after all." With those words, he pushed past Tielle and headed from the terrace.

"Was it all worth it?" Desree followed Faro from the dining room when he left.

The hallway hadn't quite cleared, yet Faro stopped and rounded on his aunt to fix her with a sneer. "You *all* laid the groundwork for this, trying to pass that garbage off like he deserved that place at the head of Dad's company. All the while you treated me like I was an outcast."

"You know you left us no choice but to treat you that way," Leo said, catching up to aunt and nephew.

"That's not all I know." Faro's voice had softened.

"Let it go," Leo urged. "No one's interested. No one's been interested for a long time. Why is it everyone loves your brother except you?"

Faro seemed stunned. "Are you really asking me that?"

"He's still your brother. Regardless," Desree said. "He's still your blood."

Faro was opening his mouth to respond to Desree when he saw Graedon rounding the corner. "My blood! My brother!" He extended a hand. "I may have been able to fall in love with Grae as deeply as the rest of you if only my father hadn't forgotten he already had a son."

* * *

Tielle followed Grae from the terrace. She traveled at a light sprint, not wanting them to leave issues unsettled between them amid so much family discord. She turned down the dining room hall to find that a crowd had gathered. Many of the breakfast attendees had found their way into the corridor.

"Faro, please don't do this," Desree appealed to her nephew, both hands clasped in a fist at her breasts. "This won't solve a thing, and you're so wrong if you think any of this will benefit you."

"You're right, Des." Faro sneered down at the woman. "In light of Grae's latest trick, I may not benefit at all from this, but it sure will make me feel a helluva lot better to bring that bastard down a few pegs."

"Faro—"

"Stop it!" Faro ordered the unidentified voice of reason in the crowd. "It's past time for everybody to cease protecting their golden boy."

Faro waited until the collective gasp had silenced within the group. "Don't be surprised. Especially when I'm very correct in my labeling. A bastard is exactly what he is!"

"Faro!"

"You're no Clegg, *Graedon!* Humph, they even gave the garbage my grandfather's name! Dad was a sex-whipped idiot who let my mother make a fool of him every time he turned around or every time she opened her legs, whichever was faster, and from what I've heard of dear old Mom—"

Leo charged for Faro, putting the younger man on his back before Faro could finish the rest of his accusations. There were screams and then several male family members succeeded in pulling Leo off while a few others helped Faro to his feet.

Faro shook off the help and pointed to Grae, who had yet to move from the spot he held in the hallway. "You're no Clegg. I doubt if Ma knew *what* your last name should be. Dad was a stupid soft heart who took her back every time she strayed."

"Lies!"

"Not lies," Faro told Steve Clegg, the cousin who had called out. "I wouldn't expect anyone my age or younger to know this. It was a secret kept by all the old folks with their whisperings and head shaking. Ma turned up pregnant and had to come clean to the husband she hadn't slept with in four months. That about right, Leo?" Faro turned a phony inquisitive stare toward the man. "That was the gist of the conversation between you and my dad. The one I overheard that day when he brought me along while you two played pool."

"You're a snake!" Des cried.

"Ken Clegg was the snake, Aunty. The man never had a kind word for me until he was fightin' with Mama, and then I was his ace. He'd spend time with me. Ball games, burger joints, taking me along when he handled business or met up with friends, like good ol' Leo." Faro grunted a laugh.

"Did your best bud tell you you're a bastard, Grae?" He shrugged. "Obviously not, but don't hold it against ol' Leo. Chances are Desree told him not to. He's as whipped as Dad was and probably even more of an idiot. At least Dad got the panties every now and then. Des still bein' a tease, Leo?"

Grae lost whatever had been restraining him. A snarl distorted his face as he charged. He made it halfway to his brother before Asia cried out and brought attention to his actions. It took twice as many men to restrain Grae as it had Leo. The group was unsuccessful at getting Grae to come to a complete stop, but they managed to slow him down enough.

"Somebody get Faro out of here!"

Meanwhile, Tielle made a desperate push to reach Grae. The bodies filling the suddenly stifling space of the corridor made that impossible.

"Grae!"

Men were shoving Grae down the hall in the direction away from his brother. Tielle was scarcely heard among the mix of devastation and outrage claiming the other voices in the air.

"Can I do anything else?" Laura asked when she opened her office door to Tielle later that evening.

"Thanks, Laura. Just don't let anybody find us in here for a while, okay?"

"On it." Laura gathered her tablet and tote bag. "I fixed you guys up with tea and pastries. I wasn't in the mood for more, but I could call down to have them send something over." She gave a look toward the food cart in her office living area.

"It'll do." Tielle's voice carried weariness as she tried massaging the kinks from her neck. "We'll call if we need anything else."

Laura replied with a sad smile and pulled the office door shut behind her. Tielle pressed her head to the cool wood, sighed and then turned to observe Desree. The woman had taken a seat in an armchair near the fireplace. Flames scorching the sides of the brick hearth provided the room's only illumination. They cast exuberant shadows upon Desree's face, emphasizing the unrest claiming her expression.

"Des?"

The woman jumped at the sound of her voice.

Tielle moved purposefully into the office. "This smells wonderful, doesn't it?" She rubbed her hands while journeying toward the food cart. "How about some tea? Do you want sugar and lemon with yours?"

"Is Grae all right?" Desree asked.

Tielle prepared the tea, though her hands were beginning to shake badly. "I haven't seen him since…earlier. The, um—the men have him locked in his suite. They kind of made it clear that no women were allowed." She set the teapot down and took a few breaths before attempting the prep once more.

"There was a lot of noise coming from inside earlier—not so much when I passed on my way down here," Tielle said. "Hopefully they've gotten him to calm down."

There was silence then with only the clink of the pottery and utensils as Tielle finished up with the tea. She added plump cinnamon rolls to saucers and then transported the goods from the cart to an end table between the chairs.

"Des?" Tielle rested her hand lightly on the woman's knee. "Talk to me. Was Faro right? About what he—what he said?"

Desree rested back in her chair. She appeared as though she might respond to the question, but there was nothing. Tielle passed Des a hot cup, folding the woman's hands about the warm porcelain. She smiled when Des blinked at the heat to her skin.

"Was he right, Des?"

"Yes." Desree spoke the word in a shudder and then bowed her head. "Yes." The word was a sob that time.

Tielle bowed her head, as well. "And you never told him."

"That's how Ken and Grace wanted it." Des's voice gained a bit of firmness. "Ken." She smiled, repeating her brother's name. "Faro was right when he said the man was a soft heart. Tough as nails in business, but a real teddy bear when it came to the family. He fell in love with Grae the day he was born—from the time he saw him, held him."

"And Faro hated that bond," Tielle guessed.

"He didn't understand it." Desree's smile was sad. "None of us did, really. We all knew Grace couldn't keep her legs closed. Humph. Faro was right about that, too. Guess our family's had one too many adult conversations in front of the kids...."

"It's rare for a man to forgive a woman once she's strayed, but Ken always forgave her. He once told me she knew he was the one who truly loved her. Talk about a sap..." Desree's smile brightened somewhat, and she shook her head. "But we never heard about Grace stepping out on Ken after Grae came."

"And so Faro had to live with knowing Grae was the link that united his parents as *he* should've done."

Des laughed heartily then. "I doubt Faro ever cared if his parents came together, much less who brought them together. It was like Leo said—he was an awful child. My mother used to say he was born under a bad moon." She shrugged. "After a while we just accepted it, and that was harder to do than accepting Grae, I'll tell you that." She waved her hand while voicing the confession.

Desree's shadowed face softened. "Grae was brightness in every sense of the word. There wasn't a soul who didn't want to be around him. As he grew up he became even more like Ken than Faro." She rested her elbows to her knees, propped her chin on the backs of her hands.

"You remember my brother," she said, not expecting Tielle to respond. "He was massive, just like Grae, and with this—this presence that just overpowered. Grae isn't as…softhearted as Ken was, but there's goodness there—kindness. As awful as Faro could be to him, Grae still loved him." Des reached for her teacup and looked to Tielle.

"You aren't the only one who wanted to make it work between those brothers. Grae wanted that, too."

"This will devastate him, you know?" Tielle's eyes glistened with tears for the man she loved. "The fact that you and Leo knew… That you all knew…"

Desree's teacup and saucer clattered when she set them aside and clenched her shaking hands. "It was the way Ken wanted it. He didn't care how Grae came to him, only that he had, and he never wanted anyone to tell Grae different. Grace certainly wasn't going to go against those wishes, and neither were any of the rest of us.

"Faro…" She sighed once her nephew's name had passed her lips. "He was always such a terrible child. Blackhearted and conniving almost from the day he could talk."

Des laughed shortly. "I can't count the times that we all sat around laughing at how things turned out. Faro was less like Ken or even Grace, for that matter. *He* was the one nobody could believe was a Clegg." Her laughter tumbled out robustly for a while and then turned into sobs. "Do you think he'll ever speak to me again, Tielle?"

"I'm sure he will." Tielle reached over to pat the woman's knee. "But he's going to want answers, and it'd be wise not to keep anything else from him."

"There's nothing else," Des swore. "At least nothing I'm keeping." She turned wet eyes to Tielle. "Do you think he'll ever forgive me?"

Tielle's answer lay in the solemnness of her expression—potent even against the firelight. Desree bowed her head and began to cry.

Sometime later, Laura found Tielle alone in her office. The firelight had dimmed, and the embers were low yet fought to regain their former glory.

"How are you?" Laura joined Tielle on the sofa facing the fireplace.

"Same as everyone else, I guess." Tielle's voice was monotone.

Laura nodded. "How'd it go with Mrs. Clegg?"

"Humph." Tielle rested her face in her hands. "I think this'll be our first retreat where people leave worse off than they were when they got here."

"Oh, I don't think so." Laura bumped Tielle's shoulder with her own. "Faro's motives were probably misplaced, but now that this is out in the open, the family can move forward."

Tielle reached over to squeeze Laura's hand. "I hope you're right, because right now I really can't see it."

It was past midnight when Tielle overcame her nervousness and decided to check in on Grae. She'd seen most of the men who had rustled him off earlier in the halls or out for a stroll or drink at the terrace bar, and she hoped the time was right to speak with her ex.

She found the door apparently closed, but upon nearing it, she discovered it was ajar.

"Grae?" She eased into the room, finding it quiet and tidy. There was no trace of Grae.

"He's gone."

She whirled around, finding Leo in the doorway.

"Maid already got the room fresh for the next guest."

"Where?" Tielle could add no more to the question.

"My guess is back to Portland." Leo stepped closer. "I'm sorry, Tielle."

Her lips pursed. "I'm the last person you should be giving apologies to. You should save them all for Grae."

Leo nodded, lowered his head. "I know, but it doesn't look like apologies are being accepted right now."

"Will you give up?" she asked.

Leo smiled. "Never. I love that kid like he's mine. We've had disagreements before. Grae always cools off after a day or two." He shrugged, looking uncertain. "I'm sure it'll take longer than a day this time."

"Well, you're welcome to stay." Tielle gave up a smile. "We won't close for the holidays until another week or so. We certainly aren't in any hurry to book our next retreat."

"Thanks," he said, grinning, "but it's probably better I head out. Some of the family left not long after Grae cleared out."

"And Faro?"

Leo muttered an expletive. "Hopefully he's taken a one-way train to hell."

Tielle studied the room Grae had used. "Do you think he'll give up on getting what he wanted out of this?"

"Not a chance. Putting this scheme in place was part of all the fun. He's been wanting to tell this for a long time. Now that the cat's out of the bag, he'll milk it for all it's worth. You can believe that."

"And where does that leave Grae in all this?"

"Angry," Leo said without hesitation. "That's the scariest part of the whole thing."

Tielle bristled at the chill that raced down her arms. "Are you scared of what he might do to Faro?"

"I'm scared of what he may do, period. The man was a terror when he lost you. That's why Asia's so upset with you."

Tielle was quiet as the image of Grae's cousin emerged in her head.

"It's not good for a man that powerful physically and businesswise to have anger issues." Leo gave Tielle a measuring look. "When you left, folks were almost afraid to e-mail him, much less talk to him."

"He came to see me." She looked around the room again. "He wanted to talk about Faro using this place for the retreat and asked how I felt about it. He seemed calm then."

Leo nodded. "You've spent a year apart. The time alone did him a lot of good, got him to see his fault in all this, but, Tielle, he was working off the assumption that you were right about Faro. That *he* was being unfair and should work harder to make things better between them. That's all out the window now. He's angry with Faro, but madder at himself for not listening to what he knew was true about his brother."

Leo quieted, and Tielle used the time to mull over his words and wonder where she resided on her ex-husband's anger meter.

Chapter 14

A fresh dusting of snow had settled during the night, but that didn't stop the retreat's guests from heading out early the following morning. The cook staff didn't need to bother with full breakfast prep, but they did supply the group with fresh coffee, Danish and bagels to provide a little nourishment for the day ahead.

Tielle kept to her office for much of the morning and didn't care if the act effectively labeled her a coward. She did busywork until the bulk of the group had set off. Armed with a mug of tea, she met Laura on the main porch.

"Think they'll recommend us to their friends?" Laura teased as they watched the last of the family clear out.

Laughter flowed softly between Laura and Tielle.

"So when do you plan to hit the road?" Laura asked once she'd sipped her tea.

"Humph. Trust me, I won't need to be bullied into taking a vacation. I'm more than ready to head someplace hot and sunny."

"Sounds fabulous, but I meant when are you hitting the road to see Grae?"

Tielle looked down into her cup. "I don't think he's in the mood to hear from me right now."

"I don't believe that." Laura sent Tielle a sidelong glance. "Not after what I've seen this past week. He still loves you, Ti. It's obvious you still love him, but the man can't even seem to move when you're in his line of sight. I don't think a man *that* in love with a woman would want to be away from her that long."

Tielle snuggled into the gray wool wrap she'd thrown on over her jeans and sweater. "This is about more than lost love, Laura," she said while taking a seat on the porch step that had been cleared of snow. "What do I say to him about this? He's insanely in love with his family, and now this. I can't even imagine what's going through his mind let alone figure out what to say to him about it."

"Maybe he doesn't need you to *say* anything." Laura rested against one of the porch columns. "Just be there."

Tielle cast a look at her. "You tryin' to get rid of me?"

"Not at all. Just trying to get you to do what you really want to be doing."

"Right. And get rid of me in the process."

Laura blew a kiss Tielle's way. "Take it how you want. Let me know if you need help packing."

Leo sat on his desk, head in hands as he prayed for an end to the incessant traffic in and out of his doors. It had been that way since his return from the retreat two weeks prior. That morning's events had merely layered more frustration to an increasingly agitating day.

"Does he hate him this much, Leo?" Simon Clegg asked. He had been overseeing daily operations of the firm while Grae and Leo attended the family gathering in Canada.

Three Cleggs stood in Leo's office. One of them had brought the morning's paper.

Leo reread the story's headline: Clegg CEO Not a Clegg.

"What's he hoping to accomplish with this?" Gerald asked. "Our clients don't care what Grae's bloodline is, only that he's making them money."

"It's not about money for Faro." Leo sighed. "He won't be happy till he's got Grae out of the company."

"He might achieve his goal." Simon took the paper. "No one's seen Grae since the trip."

"Why's this such a mission for Faro?" Wesley asked. "It's been years. Isn't there a statute of limitations on sibling rivalry?" He grinned at his brother Gerald.

Leo laughed. "Never, and Faro won't ever forgive Grae for having Ken's love."

"But that's not G's fault!" Simon ranted.

"True." Leo shrugged beneath his olive-brown suit coat. "But Grae's the only one left to pay for that, isn't he?"

"Well, Faro's mistaken if he thinks this stunt will get him back in the business and at the head of the table, besides!" Gerald swore.

"Remember, guys—" Wesley's voice softened "—Faro's had decades to stew in the unloved-child soup. Do we just put up with his antics till he brings the family all the way down?"

Again, Leo put his head in his hands. From that position he asked the most pressing question. "So who's gonna talk to Grae about this morning's paper?"

Finding Asia waiting to see her sent Tielle's teeth gritting the moment their gazes locked across the room. Starting her day with a high dose of bad blood wasn't what Tielle had expected when she arrived at her office that morning.

Tielle decided the moment had long passed for pleasantries. "I don't have the time, Asia. Actually, there never *is* time for dealing with your bull."

Asia didn't appear stunned or offended by the insult. "I deserve that and more besides for the things I've said and insinuated to your face and…behind your back."

"Gee, thanks." Tielle rolled her eyes and settled behind her desk to boot her computer.

Asia was quiet, fidgeting with the cuffs of her sweater and smoothing her hands over the arms of the chair she occupied.

"I'd offer you something," Tielle said as she got up to prepare her morning tea, "but I'm sure you have to get back on the road ASAP."

"This is about Grae."

"'Course it is."

"We haven't seen him in two weeks."

Tielle came down off some of her resistance. She returned the teapot to the beverage cart without pouring any for herself. "Is he in Portland?" Concern turned her voice faint.

"We don't even know that for sure," Asia said.

"After what happened, the guys who took Grae back to his room. What'd he say to them?"

"Not much, um… He ordered them to let him go and…*handle* Faro."

Tielle closed her eyes, understanding the word as "Grae-speak" for "do bodily harm."

"Nobody knew he'd even left that night." Asia's voice was thicker given the sob trying to claim it. "He convinced everybody he was all right and then…"

"Are you guys sure he didn't go to *handle* Faro, after all?"

"Doubtful." Asia snorted. "Especially since Faro felt well enough to share his story with the press."

"Faro," Tielle groaned while bowing her head.

"This is a nightmare," Asia sniffed.

"Did you know? About Grae not being one of you?"

"I'd heard things." Asia shook her head. "Too young to understand them and then after a while I just didn't want to know. It doesn't matter." She sniffed again and lifted her head to pin Tielle with a steady look. "Grae is part of this family, and being at the head of Clegg Marketing is where he belongs."

"Is that why you're here?" Tielle folded her arms over the ribbed bodice of her multicolored sweater dress. "Because Grae's so good in business? Making you all lots of money? He keeps you living very well, doesn't he?"

Asia's temper showed signs of life. "We have loved Grae since before he could write his name or talk. We just want him in our lives."

"And everything back like it was."

"No, Tielle. Never like it was—not like it's been for the past year." Asia left her chair and started to pace the office. "Grae's been living on the edge since he lost you. Faro's only gotten worse but with you there to—to keep the peace, keep his mind fixated and calmed by the...the love you brought to it..." She turned to face her cousin's ex-wife.

"Those of us who couldn't see that before, we—we see it now." Asia slapped her hands to her generous thighs. "Of course me, being the most bullheaded of the bunch, I saw it last."

Tielle raised her chin. "Why are you here? What do you want from me, Asia?"

"Just go see him."

"Asia—"

"Tielle, please—"

"He probably despises me as much as he does Faro."

"Not likely." Asia pursed her lips. "Chances are you're the only one he'll open his door to. Even if he isn't there—we'd appreciate you trying, Tielle."

"And what do you think I could accomplish?"

"If he simply talks to you, that'd be good."

"This is funny." Tielle shook her head, sending her thick ponytail bouncing wildly. "Pretty hypocritical for you to ask me to do something you gave me hell over when it came to Faro."

"You're right we are, but it's like I said, we've been bullheaded. We just want to know he's all right. If you're the only person he'll ever talk to, then we'll live with that." Asia moved closer to Tielle. "If you're the only person he'll ever talk to, then we'll *have* to live with that, but if you *do* talk to him, *please* tell him we love him and we never wanted this to touch him."

"Tielle, do you know what you're doing?" she asked herself as she took another breath and then rapped the door knocker to Grae's downtown Portland condominium.

"Grae? It's me—it's Tel…" She jingled the keys in her smoky-blue overcoat pocket in anticipation of tugging them out any second. There was no answer to her knock, and Tielle gave it a few moments before heading back the way she'd taken from the elevator. She'd covered a few steps when his voice resonated.

"Since when do you give up so easy?"

Tielle had turned before Grae had gotten halfway through his query. "We didn't think you were home."

"'We'?"

"Your family's very worried, Grae. They haven't heard from you in two—"

"You're running errands for my family now."

"No, I—"

"They came to you?" The barest hint of a smile curved his mouth. "They must be desperate."

"They love you, Grae."

"Damn right they do. They love me so much they couldn't bear to tell me who I really was."

"Could you blame them when the circumstances were a—" Tielle stopped herself, bowed her head.

"Were a what, Tel? A disgrace?"

She shook her head. "You can't believe that!"

"And what would you know about it?" His tone was a soft roar. "Your family didn't lie to you your whole life—pity you because of how you came to be."

"They love you, Grae."

He rolled his eyes. "There's a very thin line between love and pity. Have you ever noticed that?"

"No, Grae. I never have."

"Never, huh?" Grae stroked his beard. The silken whiskers had grown out noticeably over the past couple of weeks, giving him a more dangerous look than usual.

Tielle wouldn't let herself be unnerved by the fierceness she saw in his bronze stare or by the way his body heaved with barely harnessed rage.

It was difficult to see the full scope of the condo, what with the overhead track lighting over the bar counter being the only source of illumination. Clearly, that area of the condo had been receiving the most use.

"What?" Tielle queried in a sudden manner, having caught the tail end of the question he'd just muttered.

Grae rubbed at his jaw, trapping Tielle in the line of a repetitious raking stare. Then, turning his back on her, he went to the bar.

"Tell me about Brunch and Memories," he repeated while pouring a straight shot of gin.

"Brunch and...Memories?" She was stumped. "What about it?"

"Well—" he paused to swallow the gin in one gulp "—you were...encouraged to get me there, right?"

"What the hell are you talking—"

"Des. She told you to make yourself available to me, didn't she?"

The way he phrased the question had Tielle's cheeks burning with the images of all the ways she'd *made herself available* to Grae during their stay at the cozy B and B.

Grae stood stroking his beard again while observing his emptied glass. "Guess you just had to offer your help."

Despite his muted tone, Tielle understood what he'd said. "Grae, I did it because—"

"No need to explain, I get it. Can't go against who you really are."

"Grae, I'm here now to check on you." Heated by his insinuation, she jerked out of her coat and threw it aside, not caring where it landed. "It must've been devastating to hear what you did, but I can't see that shutting everybody out is what's best." She moved closer. "It's all right to rage in private, but there's nothing wrong with letting everyone know it upset you. It's the only way healing and forgiveness can begin."

"Forgiveness." Grae pushed the glass aside. "Has it been so easy for you to get around to that with Faro?"

"I haven't seen him."

"I don't mean since the retreat." He leaned back, folding his arms across his stunning chest. "Have you forgiven him, Tel? Forgiven him for making you waste all that time pleading his case to me when I knew all along that he had no interest in a loving, brotherly relationship?" He settled back more comfortably and cocked his head at a curious angle. "Or maybe he'd already told you that? He always seemed to be able to confide in you."

"You can't think…?" Tielle couldn't force herself to finish the question. Jaw dropping, she gaped at him.

"Did he tell you? Did he tell you what he knew about me?"

"I hope you're drunk because otherwise that'd mean you're just an idiot!" she hissed.

Grae pushed off the counter and didn't appear to be offended. "It's a fair question."

"Fair in what way?" She watched him coolly reaching for the gin and shook her head dazedly. "Unbelievable. You know, Grae, with every other insane thing going on between us, I don't have time for anything more." She turned. "Call me when you sober up. I'll be in Vancouver." She was plucked off her feet before she got within touching distance of the doorknob.

"Grae—" Her breath caught when he wouldn't budge. He crowded her against the door, and she shook her head and bristled. "You're drunk. Get off me."

He stepped back, giving her some space. "I'm not drunk. I'm not drunk. Just don't leave." He felt her breathing slow, and he glanced back at the bar. "That was my first drink today."

"Today?" she blurted.

He produced a weary smile and set his forehead to the door.

"Grae." Tielle turned to him, smoothing the back of her hand down his cheek. "Come on. Let's sit in the living room."

He waved her off halfheartedly. "That'll put me to sleep."

"All right, here." She clutched his arm and maneuvered them back to the bar area. She got him seated, intending to prepare him a cup of black coffee from the personal coffeemaker on the counter.

Grae stopped her before she could move too far. "Thanks, Tel. I'm sorry I, um, I don't know what's wrong with me."

"Stop," she soothed. "You've just had the biggest shock of your life, and the two people best equipped to help you deal with it aren't here anymore." She was referring to his parents.

Grae had no comeback, and he could only prop his elbow on the bar while he mulled over her words.

Tielle squeezed his shoulder and made another move for the coffeemaker. Again, she found herself ensnared in his grasp.

"Grae, this won't solve the problem. You don't need this." Tielle bit her lip when a moan suddenly pressured the back of her throat. Grae was treating her earlobe to slow, wet nibbles.

"I always need this," he said. "Always need it from you."

"Coffee would probably suit you better," she argued weakly.

"So you say." He didn't sound at all convinced.

His nibbles gained heat and moisture. Big hands spanned up from Tielle's waist, massaging her spine and shoulder blades before easing around to cup her breasts. Repeatedly, he flicked his thumbs across the buds imprinted beneath the material of her cotton top. Tielle gasped something needy and unrecognizable.

Grae left off his torture of her lobe to glide his nose across the silken skin below, traveling the elegant curve of her jaw down to her throat, where he began a faint suckle of her collarbone. Suddenly, he left the bar chair and took her with him. They were in the midst of a full-blown kiss by then.

Tielle clutched the neckline of his T-shirt while losing herself in the kiss that grew deeper. She wasn't sure how long they had been moving, but soon she was enjoying the feel of plush firmness of an enormous bed beneath her back. Grae's earlier fondling of her breasts had succeeded in parting the short, upturned collar of her top where the neckline already dipped into an alluring V. She squirmed, eager to be free of the shirt's confines.

Grae eased back, allowing her room to shed the top and bra. He pounced then. Hungrily, he feasted on the delicate undersides of her breasts. He divided his attention equally between the firm peaks, emitting rough sounds of satisfaction each time he drew her into his mouth.

Tielle felt his fingers skim the waistband of her panties and only then realized he'd already undone her jeans.

"Grae." She felt that she should at least put up a little

professional effort to assist him in handling the devastating blow he'd just experienced. "Wait…"

"Okay." He made no attempt to cease his sinful handling of her body.

Tielle melted into the luxurious fabric of the walnut-brown comforter. Giving in to abandon, she arched into the exquisite tugs of his lips and fingers to her nipples. His free hand moved, vanishing beneath the scrap of lace spanning her hips. Delight sent her body into a sharp spasm.

Grae only toyed with her at first, just lightly grazing his middle finger across the bud of sensitive flesh at the apex of her thighs. Then he was tormenting her with strokes to her intimate folds.

"Stop teasing," she panted, lifting her hips from the bed when he thrust the digit inside.

Weakened, Grae rested his head on her shoulder. Creamy sensation pampered his finger where it eased into her tight well, stirring and thrusting in leisurely succession. The moves had his healthy erection throbbing in anticipation of taking the place of his finger and journeying deeper.

Just then, however, he was content letting his fingers be his guide. His hips nudged hers while his imagination had its way. He ignored what sounded like the doorbell even after it had chimed through the condo one, twice, three times…

When a quiet respite was followed by what could be mistaken for nothing other than a fist pounding on a door, Grae raised his head.

"What the hell…?"

"Sounds important," Tielle whispered.

Grae emitted a rough purr. "It can wait."

Another booming series of knocks cascaded upon the door to punctuate his decision. Tielle felt a growl vibrate from Grae's chest and through hers. Then he was bolting from the bed. Tielle pushed herself up, fixing her clothes as she sat.

"Don't even think about it, Tel," Grae ordered over his shoulder as he left the room.

The command was one she had no trouble adhering to. Content, she settled down to the massive and obscenely comfortable bed. The central heating activated, and the calming sounds of rushing air filled the room. The lullaby set in motion by the warm air might have put Tielle to sleep were it not for the voices. They were low, but stirring, at first before rising in volume with clipped edges signifying tension...or anger.

Tielle perked her ears, hoping to catch more specifics amidst the rumble. Eventually, she made out two male voices—one belonging to Grae, the other to Leo.

She closed her eyes to offer a prayer for a quick end to the increasingly hostile conversation. An end didn't appear to be on the horizon. Tielle decided to fix her clothes, her movements gaining speed as the argument's volume surged. Her fingers stilled on the waistband of her jeans when she heard a door boom shut. Scrambling off the bed, she stumbled from the room and sprinted for the front of the condo.

The living room appeared in a worse state than it had when she had first arrived. Tielle saw Leo standing in the middle of the overturned chairs.

Grae was gone.

Chapter 15

"What happened?" Tielle looked from Leo to the door and back again.

"Ever heard that line about shooting the messenger?" Leo asked. "Thankfully, Grae doesn't subscribe to it. He'd rather shoot the topic of the message."

"Where is he?"

"My guess is he's gone to have a little heart-to-heart with his brother."

Tielle accepted defeat for only a second before snapping her fingers. "I may be able to catch up—"

"Ti," Leo said, getting between her and the front door, "let him go. You'll just prolong the inevitable."

"Are you serious?" She was, for a moment, speechless. "He'll kill him."

"I don't think so. Grae didn't get as far as he has by letting rage dictate his moves."

"Leo, this isn't business, it's very personal, and it has been for years." She stilled. "What'd you say to him?"

"Faro went to the press about this after all. I've been here every day hoping he'd open the door and talk to me about it. He finally did. Do I have you to thank for that?" He watched Tielle take a seat on the nearest sofa arm.

"Faro knows Grae's been…absent going on two

weeks. He's demanding the top spot at Clegg and says he's willing to take it to court," Leo shared. "If he wins, and chances are pretty strong that he could, he's already threatened to toss every one of us out on our asses."

Tielle couldn't stop herself from dwelling on the inevitable. If Grae was on the way to see his brother, he'd surely kill the man.

"I need to find him." She shoved an overturned chair out of the way.

"Honey, haven't you had enough of coming between those two?"

Tielle whirled around as though a physical force had directed her. "So you're finally around to blaming me too, huh?"

"Honey, no." Leo moved to draw her close and drop a kiss to her forehead. "You're the last person who deserves any blame for the fallout between those two, and what good has it done you? Maybe it's time to let the chips fall where they may. Only way there will be any progress, right?"

"Humph." Tielle recalled saying something similar to Grae and shrugged. "Right."

Tielle stepped out onto the porch clutching a hot ceramic mug between her hands. Inhaling, she smiled as serenity claimed her, which it had consistently and appreciatively done over the past three days.

It was hard *not* to feel secure. Especially then. She loved the retreat the closer the year churned toward its end. The parties had all cleared out, hopefully healed or, at the very least, no worse than they'd been before arriving.

She bowed her head, sipping at the soothing rose

petal and chamomile blend inside the mug. She'd been on her own going on three days. Her live-in staff had all headed off to their well-deserved vacations or to visit with friends and family for the holidays. But for her skeleton security staff, she alone remained.

There was nothing unsettling about it. Turner Estates had been home to her in one manner or another pretty much her entire life. She inhaled again, finding rejuvenation in the crisp chill. Virtually no remnants remained of the snowfall three weeks prior. The lingering chill, however, warned that it would not be the last dusting of the season.

Sipping more deeply from the mug, Tielle looked toward the dirt road cutting into the hill. She'd come out to the main porch two minutes after the call from the security booth. She'd hoped the tea would perform its usual wonders at soothing frazzled nerves. Its potency hadn't kicked in yet, and that didn't surprise her.

Despite it all, she put a shaky welcoming smile in place. She watched as Grae curved around the horseshoe drive and parked his olive-green truck at a slant.

"No police escort?" She attempted teasing, feeling her apprehension lift when he smiled.

"Don't celebrate too fast." Grae rounded the hulking vehicle he'd driven up from Oregon. "There may be some knocking on your door tonight."

"Tonight? You plan to stay that long?"

A sturdy shoulder rose on a lazy shrug before he went to the truck's flatbed and retrieved two duffel bags. "I plan to stay as long as you'll let me."

Tielle's hold on the mug tightened. She worked up another shaky smile. "You packed pretty light for a lengthy stay." She nodded toward the twin duffels.

His sly, adorable grin returned. "It's never good to assume. I figure I'll go back when I'm out of underwear." He shook one of the bulging bags for emphasis.

"Then by all means." She tucked a coarse lock behind her ear and turned. Opening one of the front double doors, she waved for him to precede her.

Grae met her on the porch and nodded. "After you," he insisted.

"I was sure you'd gone to kill him."

"You would've been right." Grae nodded.

He'd insisted on putting his bags away, knowing that once he'd taken a seat that wasn't behind the wheel of his truck, he wouldn't move for at least two hours.

"Then a good dose of common sense kicked in and I walked to the bar on the corner. Planned to get drunk instead."

"That's good…I guess." She leaned to top off their coffees.

He grunted. "It was on the way to being good—and then Leo found me."

"Grae…" She set down the coffeepot. "You can't hate him for keeping your parents' confidence. They've passed on, but those loyalties don't just disappear. Even if I didn't have a love for helping people, I think I'd try to carry on the retreat for my family anyway."

His attractive features clenched. "Not the same."

"It is." She added cream to her coffee. "It *could* be. My grandparents—my parents, for that matter—would never tell me I wasn't theirs."

Grae took his coffee bitter and black. He tossed down some of the fragrant brew and he approved of the the piping hotness burning its way down his gullet.

"Are you trying to tell me I'm lucky to have a brother—" he grimaced "—*half* brother who hates me?"

"I don't know." Idly Tielle went about sweetening her coffee. "I guess that'd depend on whether this is something you're glad to know or wish you didn't."

"Remember what you asked me in Portland?" she said after several moments of silence. "If Faro told me?"

Grae set down his mug with a clatter. "I'm sorry, Tel, for the question and the insult."

"It was a fair question."

"It wasn't."

"We were close, Faro and me."

Grae settled back to the chair he occupied near the library fireplace. "You were close to him because you're a decent person who can see goodness in the worst people."

Tielle sipped her coffee and delighted at the taste before her contentment faded. "That's not saying much for my judgment, is it?"

Grae toasted her with his mug. "Don't beat yourself up about it. You've got the best judgment of anyone I know."

Tielle studied the contents of her cup. "What about you? You always thought Faro was a snake, but you were willing to think better of him. I could see it when I asked you to give him a chance. Any regrets?"

"I tried so hard because you wanted me to." Grae chuckled, bracing his elbows to his knees.

"Oh." Again she studied the depths of the mug cradled in her lap. Faintly, the origins of laughter tickled the back of her throat. The sensation took shape on her tongue, tumbling past her lips in an enthusiastic and relieved display.

Grae took great pleasure in watching the woman he loved laughing with such rapture. In seconds, he was joining her.

Nightfall found the couple on one of the enclosed terraces enjoying drinks after a satisfying dinner courtesy of the Japanese steakhouse not far from the estate. The place wasn't exactly a takeout establishment, but the owners had no problem delivering a meal to the address that supplied some of their highest-tipping patrons.

Grae set his glass emptied of bourbon on the round wrought-iron table between the cushioned chaises he and Tielle occupied. "What you said about regrets, whether I had any?"

"Yeah?" She sipped from her half-full goblet of white wine.

"The way I let you go," he said after a lengthy silence. "The way I demanded you go unless you did what I wanted."

"At least you gave me a chance."

"I'm serious, Tel."

Her goblet joined his empty glass on the table, and she turned to face him.

"That ultimatum was bad enough, but the way we—Faro and me—tugged at you back and forth like you were a toy and we wanted you to decide who you wanted to play with… You were my wife. I should've treated you better than that."

"You know, instead of working so hard to reconcile you and Faro, *I* should've been trying to find out why you were so resistant to the idea despite those glimmers of hope I *thought* I saw in your eyes." She shrugged. "I just assumed it was some petty childhood issue between brothers. Nothing like this."

"Yeah…I thought it was some petty childhood issue, too."

"What are you gonna do now?" she asked.

"It's already done." Grae crossed his ankles. "When Leo found me the other night, I gave him my resignation."

Tielle gasped. "You can't."

"I did."

"But you—" She could barely catch the words that raced through her mind. "Who's gonna run Clegg?" She shook her head at Grae's knowing look.

"Leo can handle it over there until things settle down, but my time is done."

Tielle scooted closer to him. "Because of you, your dad's company has the kind of success he worked so hard to bring it into. Your family knows no one can top what you've done there. Not Leo and definitely not Faro."

"They lied to me, Tel. Every day, they smiled in my face, patted my back for a job well done… They played me for a fool."

"You don't believe that."

"I do."

"What about before you ever went to work for Clegg?"

Grae's upper lip curled into a snarl. "That was for my dad's sake. Couldn't upset the guy with all the money, could they?"

"You're angry." She rested her elbow on the cushioned arm of the lounge. "You have every right to be, but when you're done with that emotion, you'll put your energy on the one that's always been there—the love they have for you and yours for them." Encouragingly, she eased her hand across one of the broad forearms bared by the sleeves of the worn T-shirt carrying the emblem of his favorite pro basketball team.

Grae caught her wrist before Tielle could react. "I'd rather put my energy on you—the love that satisfies me."

Her smile was sad. "I haven't been so satisfying over the last year."

"You've been making up for it."

"Glad to hear it."

"Oh, you've still got a lot of making up to do." His hand firmed at her wrist.

"Grae—"

"Hmm." Seamlessly, he tugged her from the lounge until she was straddling his lap.

"I thought you wanted to talk?" Her question carried on an unsteady breath.

Grae's focus was on loosening the stringed bodice of the teal lounge dress Tielle had worn that night.

"I'm sure there will be talking involved." He began a slow, circular caress of a firming nipple while steadily unraveling the stark-white tassels securing the front of her dress. The strings offered teasing glimpses of plump cleavage.

Tielle bit her lip at the warm, heady sensation she felt from someplace deep.

"Don't bottle it up, Tel. I'm the only person who can hear you."

She responded with a steady laugh. "I knew I should've been more careful about who I let in my house."

"You should. A man like me could just come in and take what he wants...."

The words silenced when his lips closed over a nipple peeking through her unraveled bodice strings.

She groaned. "What kind of man are you?"

"One who can't stay away from you. One who'd do anything to keep you—preferably like this." His words were soft and shared intermittently as he gave the nipple a lengthy bathing with his tongue. His beautifully shaped lips took over next to suckle the bud dry.

Tielle arched into the act. Her fingers charted a trail over his bare forearms and the stunning breadth of his shoulders. They curved about his nape, scraping the fine, dark hair tapered there. She tried pushing more breast into his mouth, but he only seemed to want her nipple. Deliciously frustrated, she ground on his lap and smiled when he responded with a tortured groan.

Grae cupped her hip, gave a warning squeeze for her to stop. Tielle wanted him too much to cooperate. She'd been constantly reminded of the delightful interlude they'd enjoyed at his condo before family drama intervened. She was in no shape to take things slow.

Determinedly, she reached to undo his belt and slapped his hands then his chest when he tried to stop her.

"I won't last long, Tel," he warned as she resumed her task with his belt.

"Okay, then." She plied his earlobe with a wet suckle, her hand locating the prize she sought inside his jeans. She smiled at that half tortured, half satisfied groan he uttered when she gave him a naughty squeeze.

"Grae, no," she sobbed, when he clutched her waist as though he meant to pull her off his lap.

"To hell with it." He left the lounge, taking her with him. The growled words signified his defeat, his inability to resist what she so clearly wanted from him and him from her.

Grae could feel her lips curving into a smile when she

kissed his cheek and teased with a hint of her tongue. "You're not cooperating."

"I'll make it up," she taunted, outlining his mouth with the tip of her tongue. Devilishly, she evaded when he would have initiated a thorough kiss. She retraced the outline and then let her lips caress the corded column of his neck and collarbone.

Grae carried Tielle through the house like a man well familiar with his surroundings. Of course, he knew the place like the back of his hand. He'd fallen in love with his wife there.

Tielle felt no need to hang on to him. He had her secure, her bottom cradled snugly in his palms. *Her* palms ached to get beneath his T-shirt. She achieved her goal, shivering when her nails contacted the ridge of carved muscle packing his abdomen. She could feel him shiver, and she kissed his ear.

"Still ticklish?" she asked.

"I've never been ticklish."

Lightly, she trailed the honey-toned muscular expanse of his chest and felt his hands flex almost painfully on her derriere. "You're right. Not ticklish at all."

"I see there's only one way to shut you up." Impressively, he cradled her in one hand while the other cuffed her neck, his thumb tipping her chin to position her to take his tongue.

Tielle caressed his back. Her hands were still hidden beneath his shirt. She treated herself to the dual luxury of his kiss and the flex and ripple of muscle beneath her fingertips.

Graedon savored his ex-wife's incomparable talent for stroking his ego without saying a word. Her constant, breathy moans and gasping cries heightened his arrogance. He deepened the kiss as though he was intent on seeking out the source of those sensational sounds.

He took a back stairway two steps at a time. The path took him right to the floor of Tielle's room, and they were crossing the threshold within minutes.

In a show of finesse, Grae took the liberty of drawing up the folds of Tielle's dress until the material bunched at her hips—all while he held her.

"Take this off," he told her.

She pulled the garment over her head and let it drift to the floor. Wearing only the panties he'd seen fit to keep her in, Tielle suddenly found herself tossed to the center of the bed. She supported her weight on her elbows and watched him. Lips parted, she had the look of a woman panting for the tasty morsel in her sights.

Grae reached behind his neck, gripping the neckline of the T-shirt and dragging it over his head to reveal the awesome plane of torso beneath.

Her smile reflected appreciation when he sent his sweats to the floor, revealing the fact that he wore nothing more.

"Impressive." She sighed.

A lazy shrug accompanied his lopsided grin. "I try." He took time to apply protection and then crawled his way up her body until he joined her on the bed.

Still bracing her weight on her elbows, Tielle watched him come close. Her lashes batted, promising to close when she felt his skin bare next to hers. She whimpered out her delight over the sensation of their bodies caressing.

Grae mastered her mouth with another probing kiss, simultaneously using his sex to invade hers.

"Look at me," he told her.

She obliged with no small amount of difficulty. All she wanted was to close her eyes, to intensify her focus on the way he stretched her so magnificently.

"Why'd you make me wait for this?" she purred. Again, her eyes narrowed, and he "punished" her disobedience with a thrust that sent him impossibly deeper.

"Terrace would've been fine."

"I've already had you there."

Her walls clenched about his driving erection, and she settled to her back. "Lots of rooms in this house. You haven't had me in all of them."

"That's about to change." He kissed her as if to seal the promise.

Tielle would've wrapped her legs about his back then, but Grae kept her thighs spread so she could welcome every inch of his penetration.

Ragged curses slipped past his lips ever so often when that penetration promised his climax sooner than he wanted it. He could've taken her all night, listening to her heightened cries, watching her lovely face expressing pleasure when he made her orgasm… She felt amazing, had always felt amazing the way she sheathed him. How he had survived their separation, he would never know. He only knew that he wanted an end to it.

Tielle rested her arms above her head, bringing her already pert breasts to a higher level. Grae couldn't help himself. The double treat of being buried inside her while keeping her taut nipple captive inside his mouth brought him to abundant release some minutes later. The persistent throb of his need filling the condom coaxed Tielle into her second orgasm.

She chanted Grae's name as though she was thanking him. He collapsed atop her, unmindful of whether he crushed her.

Tielle didn't mind at all.

Chapter 16

As she had for the past several mornings, Tielle woke content and decadently toasty thanks to the unyielding slab of muscle at her back. Smiling, she burrowed deeper, wanting more of the heat she was being treated to.

The move caused her bottom to nudge the stiff ridge of flesh below Grae's waist. "Oops." Her murmur mixed with laughter, and she heard Grae's voice rumble seconds later.

"I hope I get more than an 'oops.'"

"Well, what more do you want?" She faked innocence and got her answer when his finger enacted a sensuous dalliance with her clit. Moving lower, he massaged the dark petals of flesh guarding her sex. Tielle turned her face into the pillows, softly moaning Grae's name while opening herself to his touch.

Curious fingers explored her moistened core, and Tielle added a subtle yet indulgent arch to her back. She flexed her inner muscles to engulf more of the finger he stirred inside her.

The bedside phone rang.

"Thought we said no phones?" he grunted while feathering kisses across her shoulder blades and nudging coarse tresses to bare more space for his lips to explore.

Tielle could barely form words due to a persistent need to gasp. She was savoring the satisfaction of two fingers then. "It's not my cell," she moaned and glared over at the ringing phone.

"Where's the phone cord?"

"Why?"

"Because I'm gonna rip it out of the damn wall."

"No need for violence." Knowing the threat was serious, Tielle moved to answer. She almost wished she hadn't after greeting Leonard Cartright on the line.

Grae eyed the phone as if it were plague-ridden when Tielle said Leo wanted him. "This is your fault," he grunted.

"I know," she said, keeping the receiver pressed to her cleavage, "but he doesn't sound so good."

Grae stroked his beard, muttered a curse and took the phone. "I don't have time for this," he told the man on the other end of the line.

Tielle watched Grae handle the call. His responses began harshly and became more so as the call went on. She scooted toward the bed's edge, intending to give him a little privacy. Grae cradled the phone against his shoulder and dropped his free hand on the covers to block her escape. Moments later, he was reaching over Tielle to slam the phone back to its receiver.

"What was that about?" she managed despite having her breathing substantially stifled by Grae's weight.

He felt around beneath the bed. Locating the phone cord, he yanked it from the wall socket. "Listen to me next time," he said.

"What happened?"

"Never mind." The words were faint. He nuzzled his

very nice face between her breasts, ready to continue what they'd started before the call.

Tielle set her hands to his shoulders, pressing with all her strength even though Grae didn't budge an inch. Finally, she resorted to thumping at the iron wall of his chest.

"Hell." He rolled his eyes at last, acknowledging the persistent blows. He rolled to his side of the bed, used a forearm to cover his eyes. "Same ol' crap," he muttered. "'Come back, Grae, just for a while. Forget about that nasty business in Canada and get back to making us all that money.'"

"Leo wouldn't say that." Tielle propped herself on her elbow and watched him. "What'd he want?" She nodded once a minute of silence had passed without an answer. "Bedtime's over," she decided.

Grae stopped her with an arm across her middle. "They want me back. Leo says it won't be long. Just for the interim until they find somebody."

"Somebody besides your brother. Leo sounded pretty desperate."

"Yeah...." Grae dug the heels of his hands into his eyes.

"You know you have to go back."

"I only know I want to be where you are."

"I'll go with you." She clutched the arm he'd just dropped over her hip.

Grae was already shaking his head. "I don't want you involved anymore." He gave her a disbelieving look. "Why would you want to be? Most of 'em didn't show an ounce of regret when we divorced."

"I just think you should go back." She raised a shoulder. "We should be there for the ones who *did* show regret." She brushed her thumb at the bend of his elbow. "Right or wrong, you've never hidden from a confrontation, never allowed anything to stop you from doing what you thought was best."

"Like forcing you to walk away from our marriage."

She smiled. "I said 'right *or* wrong.'"

Grae forced a smile through his scowl.

Tielle scooted closer. "No matter how angry you are, you can't just leave them to fend off Faro and his plans for payback." Suddenly angered by the thought of it, Tielle flopped to her back and pounded the covers beneath her fists. "He'd probably sell off the company just to spite your father for loving you."

"What?" Grae's scowl cleared.

"Well, he's always been an angry man," she said matter-of-factly. "That always came through loud and clear. I thought it was just all the stress between you guys, but he's vengeful, Grae. Are you okay leaving a company you helped to build at the mercy of someone so reckless?"

Two afternoons later, Leo Cartright looked like a man saved from the grips of a terrible fate when he found Grae in the main conference room.

"I thought they were joking when they said you were here to see me."

Grae stood and shook the hand Leo offered. "I'm not here for work."

Leo's exuberance faded. "But I thought—"

"How soon can we get the board and executive officers assembled?" Grae interrupted.

"Shouldn't take long. Mostly everyone's somewhere

on the park today. If we hustle…should have everybody here in a couple of hours."

Grae nodded. "Make it happen."

"Can you give me a hint about the meeting?" Leo spread his hands. "You've already given your resignation, but you say you're not back to work, so I guess you're not here to make the announcement we all wish you would."

"Just get everybody here and you'll have your answers."

Leo nodded, turning to leave the room.

"Leo?" Grae called. "Make sure Faro's here for this."

Leo was true to his word. After the brief discussion with Grae, he and his staff spent the next hour or so arranging the early-afternoon meeting. The rumble of mixed conversation settled to a dull roar when Graedon Clegg arrived. The room didn't go totally silent until Faro walked in some five minutes after his brother. The man offered no greetings to anyone in the room and merely spread his hands toward Grae in a *What now?* gesture.

"Thanks to everybody for getting here on such short notice," Grae said. "I know you're all aware that I've given my resignation, which leaves us in the vulnerable position of being without leadership." He looked to Faro and saw that the man's eyes had taken on the hungry gleam they adopted when he smelled blood in the figurative sense.

"I know my half brother is interested in running the company and he'd have a very good case for doing so, as we all know. Ken Clegg's will calls for a family member to be one of the chief executives. The duty of selecting the leadership is in the board's hands if no suitable family member is available."

Faro's eyes virtually glowed then in anticipation of Grae urging the board to give him the power that was his birthright.

"To have Ken Clegg's son, his *real* son, at the head of the business he grew is the best choice, and one that Ken would have supported wholeheartedly. Unfortunately, I'm not Ken Clegg's real son. *More* unfortunately, his real son has made company moves that have gone against codes of conduct in the Clegg business plan as well as his father's own will."

The gleam in Faro's eyes took on a venomous sheen, and he stepped forward to dispute.

"You tried to sell us out, Faro," Grae said before the man could give voice to his argument. "You hated Dad for letting me run the company. You hated him for loving me. It made you so mad you were hell-bent on destroying everything he treasured. You made promises—verbal and written—to sell the company upon your assignment as CEO. The land deed would've helped secure that position once you'd ousted me. With that power, not to mention being a *blood* relative, you could've done it."

"You—"

"It was fortunate that your intended buyer was one of integrity. They came to me, wanted to confirm you had the authority to make such an offer. Following a very interesting conversation that included the details of your written offer, I e-mailed the contents of it to everyone in this room."

"Bastard."

Grae smiled. "That may be, but *our* mother's marriage to our father still makes me a Clegg. That, combined with my capacity as CEO, gives me the power to have you removed. It'd be in your best interest to drop any plans you have for legal action. The courts may not look too favorably on your actions—ones we may be able to prove as illegal in their own right."

"Illegal?" Faro was stunned.

"Think about it, Faro. You can leave here and go home, or we can take it to court where your chances of going to jail could be a high possibility." Grae raised his hands toward Faro. "Floor's yours."

Free to speak, Faro declined the offer. Instead, he shot the cuffs of his pristine black suit and left the room. Once silence held just shy of half a minute, faint origins of applause began until the room was alive with cheers.

Several rushed the front of the room to shake hands with Grae and slam hearty pats to his back and shoulders. Grae found he wasn't immune to the good cheer filling the room, and soon he was grinning as broadly as everyone else.

Leo approached finally to offer his hand. "Thank you."

Grae accepted the shake. "Just keeping my word to Dad. I promised to protect the company."

Leo's expression grew stern. "Ken *was* your father, Grae. In every way that mattered."

Still clutching Leo's hand, Grae nodded, squeezing the man's forearm and pulling him into a hug. "I know that."

"I think a lot of drinks are in order!" Leo was again his jovial self when he and Grae pulled apart. "Let's meet in the exec lounge! Join us?" he asked Grae.

Grae nodded. "I can't stay long. Another stop to make."

Tielle was setting freshly folded napkins on the coffee table when the bell sounded. "I got it!" She sprinted for the foyer, opening the door to Grae. "How'd it go?" she asked.

Grae pulled Tielle close, just needing to be fortified by the nourishing powers of her hold before making any attempts at speech. The drive to his aunt's home from Clegg had given him time to reflect on the meeting earlier that day. Those reflections were ones he hoped to soon tuck away in the far recesses of his memory.

"It didn't go well—" he allowed a little space between himself and Tielle "—but the company's secure."

"And Faro? You think he'll let it go at this?"

"If he's smart, he will. And we both know how smart he is, right?" Grae pulled Tielle into another squeeze, dropping a kiss to her ear in the process.

"Does she know I'm here?" He peered past Tielle's shoulder.

"I'm pretty sure she does. She's been cooking like crazy all day." Tielle reached around Grae to close the front door of Desree's home.

"Des?" Tielle gave Grae's hand a few reassuring squeezes and tugged him from the foyer.

Desree waited in her living room. Obviously unnerved, she squeezed a white dishcloth in her hands.

"Look who's here." Tielle left Grae just inside the grand living room drenched in late afternoon sun. She went to check the casserole dishes that Des had placed on the long coffee table. "This looks fantastic!" she said of the macaroni and cheese casserole, greens, wild rice, fried chicken and egg custard pie Des had prepared for dessert.

The woman had toiled over the late supper since Tielle had called to tell her Grae would be stopping by after the meeting at Clegg. Tielle left off listing the meal when she saw Grae make the first move. He crossed to Des, taking the dishcloth from her hands and tossing it to an end table. He smothered her hands in his much larger ones and kissed her forehead. Then he pulled her into a crushing hug.

Desree's muffled, happy cries filled the room as her arms shot around Grae. Her hands rushed up his back to clutch and squeeze him to her.

Tielle blinked, realizing tears were spiking her lashes when she heard the unexpected sounds of Grae's sobbing.

"He was someone Grace picked up in a bar." Desree grimaced. "It didn't take much for her to step out—Ken not complimenting a new hairstyle or the way she looked in a dress were usually good reasons. She didn't even know the man's last name."

"How could she be sure he was the one?" Grae asked slowly.

"She told me the day she found out she was pregnant. Ken had flowers and a new diamond choker on her bed pillow. It was her birthday. She thought he'd forget. The fact that he remembered… It shook her up good."

Grae bowed his head and cursed.

"What she'd done, the result of it and then Ken's sweet birthday gift—guess it all just drove everything home, and she needed to talk." Des fiddled with the scalloped edge of the cloth napkin on her lap. "I honestly believe she never looked at another man besides your father after that last…"

Des sighed. "Ken…after he got over the shock that his wife was pregnant by another man, he did what he thought was best. He got the adoption proceedings put in place for when you came. He didn't want whoever the mystery father was to suddenly discover Grace had his child and was married to a multimillionaire besides.

"I wish they'd never told me any of it." Des closed her eyes. "Grace was in bad shape, though, needed someone to confide in, and I…I was the only one she trusted. She had no other family, her parents were gone and she was an only child.

"My brother told me nothing till years later when he asked me to hold that deed. He trusted Leo and me the most. Since Leo was already helping him with the business…"

Desree seemed to shiver on her end of the sofa she shared with Grae during the meal. "It wasn't until after Faro said he'd overheard that conversation that I wondered. Ken was a smart man. He had to pick up on Faro's ways. I think the child only got worse after he heard. I think that's why Kent gave me the deed. He knew I'd never let it go, never use it as a bargaining chip the way Faro…" She dissolved into tears. "I'm sorry. I never should've let him guilt me into doing what I knew I shouldn't." She turned tear-filled eyes to Grae.

He moved closer, kissed her cheek. "You did exactly what my father wanted—to protect the family. The way he protected me from any lowlife who may've come snooping around in hopes of any advantages being my biological father might grant him. *You* protected the family from any known or unknown threats later."

"Ken told me you weren't his when he came to me about the deed. Faro was the oldest, so it was logical that he'd be the one to lead, but Ken saw there was a chance Faro wasn't meant to be the one." Des used the corner of the napkin to dab at her eye.

"He wanted someone outside the company to be able to step in if that wasn't the case." She smiled over at Tielle, who sat across from them. "Ken knew I loved this little rug rat from the day he popped out."

She inclined her head toward Grae. "He knew I loved him just like he did, and with a love like that, he knew I'd protect what could one day be his."

"You did."

Des smiled at Grae's words. "Not very well." She looked his way. "I never wanted you to know about any of this. Besides me and Leo, the only others who knew were Barry, Frank and Asia's mother, Clara, who's been dead many years. We all loved you like you were our own, and you made that very easy each day you continued to grow into such an incredible man."

She looked toward her lap. "I'm sorry for not telling you. We denied you that right, and we're sorry. We hoped Ken would tell you before he died, and when he didn't we…we just didn't think about how to handle it. We never meant to deceive you. We just didn't know what to do."

"Shh…" Grae shook his head and brushed a rolling tear from Desree's cheek. "There's only one thing to do, you know?"

Desree blinked, waiting.

"We forget it." Grae gave his aunt a wink that encouraged her to smile.

Not only did Desree smile, she laughed and cried in

unison, throwing herself against Grae and clutching him in a suffocating embrace.

From her chair opposite the sofa, Tielle laughed and cried as well.

Vancouver—One Week Later...

"You're about to surpass me as Brunch and Memories's best customer, you know? What'd you have to buy to secure a private dining room?"

Grae demolished the last morsel of apple cobbler from his dessert bowl. "I told them we had a special occasion to celebrate."

Tielle sipped her wine. "So how long are we gonna milk this celebration thing?"

Following the late supper with Des, which had ended on a delightful note, the Cleggs had launched into a weeklong joyfest. Grae had dined out, barbecued and cocktailed with virtually every member of his family. Everyone wanted the chance to make amends for the awful events of recent weeks.

"We can still milk it a little longer. Still got some things to celebrate."

Tielle laughed, but she stopped when Grae set a tiny white saucer in the middle of the small candlelit table they shared in the dim, elegant room. In the center of the saucer was a brilliant silver hand that supported a blinding square-cut diamond.

Her jaw dropped, and, after what seemed an eternity, her eyes lifted to his face.

Grae propped his fingers to his brow and studied her knowingly. "I hoped the retreat would give me the chance to prove I wasn't the same man who forced you to change who you are or lose me. I know that who you are is who I fell in love with, and she means everything to me."

He tapped his fingers on the saucer's edge. "I know we have a long way to go, but unless you tell me it's hopeless, I don't plan on letting up until my ring's on your finger and my last name is behind your first again. If you'd like to give me your answer, I wouldn't mind."

"Wow," Tielle could only manage.

His easy expression clouded. "Please tell me it's not too late."

"Are you for real?" Her eyes sparkled with moisture. "It's never been too late. I stayed with Des a week after the divorce was final, hoping you'd come to say you'd made a mistake and that you wanted me again."

"Tel." Grae sighed, leaving his chair to come round and lean on the edge of the table. He pulled her up against him. "I always wanted you. Somehow I was dense enough not to realize how much until I lost you. I love you, Tielle."

"I love you." She smoothed her hands across his shoulders, powerful and sturdy beneath an oak-colored suit coat. "And I'd like to try something you suggested to Des a week ago."

He watched her curiously.

"Unless you're devoted to dissecting, analyzing and apologizing for every awful part of the last year, how about we just forget it? I don't know about you, but I can think of a lot better memories we can make."

Grae toyed with the lengthy sleeve of her crimson toga dress. "Does that mean you're ready to give me an answer?"

"The answer is yes, Graedon Clegg. The only question is when." Tielle spoke her question against her fiancé's mouth.

"You need to be sure, Tel. Remember, I'm unemployed at the momentÁ."

"I wouldn't call consulting with Leo about Clegg unemployed. Do you think you can hold off going back to the office till after the honeymoon?"

"No need." He gathered her closer. "The great thing about consulting is you can do it anywhere. So if you think I'd leave you in Vancouver even for a day to go sit up in an office, you're out of your mind."

"Do you mean…?" Her gaze narrowed. "You'd really consider staying?"

"Done more than consider it, Tel. I've decided. As CEO, it was my right to name my successor. Leo's more than capable, and when he's had enough, we'll put someone in charge who's equally capable."

"Sounds too good to be true." She shook her head even as she smiled.

"There's a catch." He outlined her plump mouth beneath his thumb. "As much as I love Turner Estates, I have enough memories of the place to last a lifetime. How 'bout we find our own estate?"

Her smile brightened. "To fill with our own *better* memories."

He kissed the tip of her nose. "For the rest of our lives, Tielle. For the rest of our lives."

* * * * *

Can he convince her to take another chance on love?

ESSENCE BESTSELLING AUTHOR

GWYNNE FORSTER

McNEIL'S *Match*

After a bitter divorce, twenty-nine-year-old Lynne Thurston is faced with the prospect of not knowing what to do with the rest of her life. Once a highly ranked pro tennis player, she gave it all up six years ago when she got married. Now with nothing else to lose, can she make a comeback on the tennis circuit? Sloan McNeil is a businessman who wants to convince Lynne that she still has what it takes… both on *and* off the court!

"Caring and sensitive…FLYING HIGH is a moving story fit for any keeper shelf."
—*RT Book Reviews*

Available September 2014 wherever books are sold!

H HARLEQUIN®
™ www.Harlequin.com

KPGF1590914

Is it a summer fling...or the beginning of forever?

ESSENCE BESTSELLING AUTHOR

DONNA HILL

FOR YOU I *Will*

After ten years of service as an E.R. chief at a New York City hospital, Dr. Kai Randall decided to trade her scrubs for a calmer existence in Sag Harbor Village. Still, a photo she snapped of a handsome, solitary stranger continues to haunt her. But that's nothing compared to how she feels when she comes face-to-face with the man from her dreams, Assistant District Attorney Anthony Weston. Although Anthony's life is in turmoil, could the soul-stirring passion they share be the beginning of a new life together?

"Yum! This novel in the Sag Harbor Village series is smooth and sexy like dark chocolate!"
—*Book Reviews* on *Touch Me Now*

Available September 2014 wherever books are sold!

REQUEST YOUR FREE BOOKS!

2 FREE NOVELS PLUS 2 FREE GIFTS!

KIMANI™
ROMANCE

Love's ultimate destination!

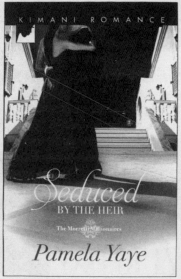

They are political
rivals…until the
doors are closed!

SECRET SILVER
Nights

ZURI DAY

Nico Drake dreams of one day becoming governor of his state.
First item on his agenda? Beating his newest mayoral challenger,
Monique Slater. She has big plans for their small town, and they
don't include falling for her sexy political rival. Keeping their
sizzling relationship under wraps while running against each other
is a tight rope act. But the voters convince Nico that there are no
losers when it comes to love.

The Drakes of California

"Day's love scenes are fueled by passion and the
tale will keep readers on their toes until the very end."
—*RT Book Reviews* on *Diamond Dreams*

HARLEQUIN®
TM www.Harlequin.com

*Available September 2014
wherever books are sold!*

KPZD3700914